JACK & EVA

FRANCES DALL'ALBA

Poinsettia
Publishing

ALSO BY FRANCES DALL'ALBA

For Dr Karen Coombes & Neil McLaughlan

CHAPTER 1

Eva Stamford's phone buzzed in the side pocket of her khaki pants. She slid it out to find Dr Karen's name flashing on the screen. She replaced the deodorant on the shelf and walked outside.

"Karen, hi, what's up?" The warm midday sun tingled Eva's arm as she raised the phone to her ear. The hint of summer was just around the corner.

"We have an unharmed tree roo in the wrong place. Where are you?"

"At the chemist. Where is it?"

"Thank goodness for that. It's at the local hardware store. The owner phoned Pete at the National Parks office. I just got off the phone with him. I'm down on the coast, so I'm not close enough to help."

"Don't stress, I'm onto it. I'll be there in exactly three minutes."

"Great. Let me know how the little guy goes."

"I will," Eva assured her. "I'll talk to you later."

Eva slid her phone back into her pocket and made for her vehicle. Dr Karen, who owned and ran the Tree Roo Rescue

Park, didn't have to ask her if she had the necessary gear in the back of her white 4WD ute. It went without saying. With it parked only metres away on the street, the local hardware shop was literally around the corner. As traffic jams weren't a thing in the small town of Malanda, there'd be nothing to hold her up.

She drove down the newly resurfaced street, and admired the brand-new mural on the side of the hardware store. Whenever she spotted the giant tree kangaroo filling much of the wall, her heart always soared. The animal captivated the most attention on the mural—and so it should! This rare kangaroo species, which looked more like a giant possum, was only found in the rainforests of the Atherton Tablelands, and a lot of Australians didn't even know they existed.

She indicated left and parked in front of the bright aquamarine hardware store. Its colour was an optimistic spot on the regular dreary and drizzly days in Malanda. The cool, wet days were perfect for her tree kangaroos but not always helpful when she needed to get out into the weather and do her job.

Eva got out of the ute and went to her toolbox. She grabbed a face shield, clear glasses, two pairs of long heavy-duty cloth gloves, a hessian capture bag and a medium-sized animal crate. With her arms full, she headed for the front door. The sound of the door buzzer announced her arrival.

Dave, the owner, gave her a cheerful smile. The smell of paints mingled with treated timber always bombarded her senses when she entered the shop. It reminded her of turpentine and the long-ago times she spent helping her dad with painting and renovations around their home. Her father smiling with his cheeks pushed down by his safety goggles and his trusty radio playing in the background as he hummed along to his favourite Eagles songs.

"Hi Eva, that was quick," Dave said, appearing from the back of the store.

"I was only down the street when Karen rang, so you're in luck today."

The few customers in the store were whispering, trying not to startle the roo. She asked Dave, "Do you know how it got in?"

"We only opened an hour ago, and I can pretty much guarantee it wasn't already in the shop. I'm guessing it was perched in the tree out the front and hopped in not long after I rolled up the front trade door."

Eva peered around a stacked shelf of paintbrushes. "Where is it now?"

"Just go through to that aisle over there." Dave pointed to the aisle running along the far wall. "There are a couple of customers keeping an eye on it. It's found a very comfortable spot in the plumbing section. I reckon we should call him Kenny."

Eva chuckled at the reference to the popular Australian character and followed Dave's directions.

Dave trailed her towards the rear of the hardware store. "I thought it was some clumsy customer dropping lots of plumbing fittings onto the floor. I couldn't believe it when I saw him."

"It can't see too much, poor thing." Eva crept into the aisle and paused. There was a slight tremble in its front paws; its long tail was stationary.

"Blind?" Dave whispered from behind her. "Then how did it find its way into such a comfortable spot?"

"Trust me on this one, Dave. It's probably more just luck that he didn't get run over before finding his way inside."

Eva snuck down the aisle on silent feet. She held a finger to her lips to show the customers they should continue keeping their voices down. The chance sighting of a tree kangaroo would enthral them, just as it did for Eva. It didn't matter how often she was around them, the excitement factor never changed. Such an amazing animal and so little understood. And if the community didn't do something to protect their rainforest habitat, it was in danger of becoming a threatened species.

"I need some help. Who'd like to volunteer?" Eva whispered in the confined space of the plumbing aisle.

"I can," came a gruff voice.

Eva lost her traction for a moment when a man rounded the other end of the aisle. Azure-blue eyes and a serious face greeted her. She gulped and quickly swallowed. Wow! She'd lived in Malanda for nearly five years and had never seen this bloke around. It was hard for someone who had sworn off men recently to ignore the good looks and glossy polish of the new man in town.

Two facts collided in her brain, and she realised who the man might be. "Sure." She switched her attention back to the tree roo and handed the man the animal cage. "Dave," she whispered over her shoulder, "can you close all the doors in case this baby leaps its way out onto the street?"

"Will do," he whispered back, his quiet footsteps disappearing towards the front of the store.

"Could the rest of you except, ahh …" She glanced at the stranger.

"Jack," he said.

She gave him a tight smile. So, her suspicions had been correct. "… except Jack, step right back. These little guys have sharp claws, and I don't want anyone in the way."

She waited until the onlookers moved to the other end of the aisle, phones in hands, capturing every second.

Taking a moment to study the roo, she noted the healthy

look of its brown-to-gold-tinged fur and overall appearance of good health. She did a quick check to confirm he was a male roo, before looking for any visible scars or blood. It was a miracle he hadn't been run over getting into town. Her heart melted whenever she was this close to a tree kangaroo. Right now, she desperately wanted to wrap her arms around him and keep him safe.

But common sense prevailed. If startled when held, it could easily gouge her eyeballs out. "Okay, Jack, put these gloves and safety glasses on." A hint of fresh pine aftershave wafted near her nose as she handed over the gear. She swallowed and licked her lips for good measure. Jack was no ordinary man just passing through town. Of that, she was now certain.

"The animal is most likely blind," she whispered to Jack. "I need you to hold open the door of the cage. If I'm lucky and get the roo into the capture bag, I'll release it immediately into the cage."

Jack gave a quick nod. They donned their face shields and gloves. With the bag open and ready, she edged towards Kenny, nestled amongst stormwater bends and fittings, trying not to step on the plumbing connectors strewn across the floor.

She held her breath as she inched closer. Kenny appeared none the wiser to her movements, confirming there was some blindness. Within seconds and in one swift action, the bag was over its head and down its body, not giving Kenny a moment to feel startled. She tightened the drawstring, her arms straining against the weight in the bag. The roo was probably stunned, its adrenaline pumping as fast as hers. She had to act immediately before it realised it was confined.

"Okay, are you ready, Jack?" Eva sat on her knees in front of the cage on the floor.

He nodded quickly, squatting to hold the spring-loaded door of the cage open. Their eyes met, his full of concentration and apprehension. She positioned the bag's opening near the cage entrance and slowly undid the drawstring. The tree kangaroo didn't waste another minute and scurried out of the bag.

Only when the cage was secured did she allow herself to breathe again. This sort of rescue didn't usually go wrong, and the worst she experienced in the past was a gashed arm. Luckily today, there'd be no blood to clean up.

"I'm Eva by the way and thanks for helping out," she said as Jack stood with the cage in hand.

"I can carry it out for you," he replied.

Ohhh, even the sound of his deep voice was sexy. But time to stop thinking these thoughts before she did something goofy. She clambered onto her feet. At twenty-nine, she should be able to handle herself around an attractive man. "Thank you. I'll let Dave know Kenny is safe."

Jack bobbed his head once, his face not once breaking into a smile. Dark and broody were the vibes he emitted. Not her type and not what she'd been expecting. Good lord, what was her type? She shook her head and made her way to the front counter. There didn't seem to be anyone in her past who could keep up with her and her one passion in life—saving the Lumholtz tree kangaroo.

Jack drove his top-of-the-range Toyota LandCruiser carefully down the rainforest-covered, rutted drive. At least it wasn't steep and slippery. He would have to lay gravel to make it easier in the wet season … if he held onto the property for that long.

Nothing could stop the persistent pounding in his chest. Thirteen years was a long time. Had the rainforest staked its claim on the land by webbing its foliage closer and tighter together? Was it telling him something? He clearly remembered more light filtering through the trees on the afternoons that his parents made him walk the four kilometres between his home and school. Unlike most children, he was more afraid of what he found at home than anything that could come out of the forest.

Time would never heal that.

He turned the last corner and braked, stopping in front of the house. The once stunning Queenslander his grandfather built didn't look to be in too bad shape. An open verandah — minus the solid sturdy table and chairs he used to do his homework on — ran the length of the frontage. Peeling white paint covered the balustrade he remembered so well. A three-step rise in the middle of the house led to the front door. Behind which were the bedrooms to the right and the kitchen, living room and laundry to the left.

While the house and front yard looked cared for and neat, he didn't doubt that lots of overdue maintenance would be required. Nothing he couldn't afford if he wanted to. He had vague plans, and being constantly reminded of his childhood wasn't one of them. He wasn't sure exactly what to do about that problem.

Looking closer at the yard, he was surprised that someone had mowed the lawn and trimmed back the shrubs. The midmorning sun took that moment to peek through the grey clouds and bask the mould-splotched roof in its rays. It stirred odd feelings of resentment that he was forced to leave his home all those years ago. Which surprised him as there were few happy memories to hold onto.

An iridescent-green Cairns Birdwing fluttered past,

landing on his side-view mirror. His mother had once said she attracted butterflies. Was this his mother watching over him? She promised him his grandfather's property would one day be his, and she delivered.

But at what cost? And did it matter anymore?

He swallowed the huge wad of emotion caught in his throat and got out of the car. Maybe it mattered a little. His only contact with anyone in this town over the years had been with the friendly solicitor who knew him when he was young. The solicitor took care of his mother's affairs and collected the rent from his father. Was this tidy welcome his doing?

He took his first tentative step towards the wrap-around verandah and filled his lungs with the intoxicating smell of rainforest—wood, soil and damp moss. It brought back a host of memories. To the days when his young legs took him away from the house, the shouting only dimming when he reached the tree line. Once there, he would take hesitant steps until his curiosity had him sifting through the undergrowth to see what lived there. Some days, it was all he needed to switch off from the violence nearby.

His ear cocked to the sound of an approaching car. Why would anyone be on the road? Before registering much, he recognised Eva's ute he'd put the animal cage into only a couple of hours earlier.

She braked abruptly beside his car and hopped out. "Hi, Jack."

Why was she here? He remained silent, watching her rifle through some gear in the ute's toolbox. She donned the same long gloves and perched clear safety glasses on her button nose.

"Just checking my babies. Sorry to bother you, I won't be too long," she called, heading for the treeline.

Her babies? On his property?

On short, trim legs, she strode towards the back of *his* property, oblivious as his jaw dropped. What the heck? Had someone else made claim to the property? For eight months it had sat vacant while Jack debated what to do with it. Had the locals claimed it as their own?

He gritted his teeth and followed. She moved like a pocket rocket, someone with too much energy. It'd drain him in minutes if he let it, but he pinned his gaze on the thick ponytail of honey hair that hung halfway down her back, swishing from side to side like a horse's tail, determined to sort this out. "Eva!"

She looked over her shoulder, putting her finger across her mouth to silence him. *What the—?*

She followed what appeared to be an invisible track with confident steps, a sure sign she'd done this many times before.

Not wanting to lose sight of her, he almost ran into her back when she halted.

"Look up," she whispered.

He did, and perched on nearly every branch were about a dozen tree kangaroos of various sizes. Momentarily stunned, he couldn't understand how he'd spent seventeen years of his youth here and had never seen a single tree roo. Had they appeared out of nowhere? Had they only been discovered recently?

"Aren't they beautiful?" she murmured, her head tilted to the rainforest canopy.

What? This was enough to snap Jack out of his trance and back to the current situation. He wasn't going to agree to anything. Firstly, she was trespassing on his property while he was supposed to be de-stressing and deciding what to do with it. This place was a world away from the life he'd created. But his last girlfriend had told him he needed to find a quiet space and empty all the pain and jumbled thoughts he couldn't seem to talk about.

Her words had motivated him to take a year away from work and sort himself and the property out. He couldn't keep putting it off. "I'm the new owner of this place. I'd appreciate it if you didn't trespass. There must be another way to get to this area."

Unperturbed by his response, she continued as if he hadn't spoken. "I rescued some of these as joeys," she whispered. "We've given them time to grow before releasing them back into the wild. How good is this, Jack? Look at how happy they are."

Happy? How did one determine how goddamned happy a tree kangaroo was?

Her shoulders seemed to drop with relief. "Come on, I'll make us a cup of tea. I have a hot water flask." With the same rapid abruptness as her arrival, she rounded him and picked her way out of the rainforest.

Confusion marred his brow. He couldn't imagine anyone befriending his hostile father—a man who'd never been too far from a drink or using his fists. There had to be an explanation. "Are you a friend of the solicitor who sorted the legal side of the property?"

"Everyone is friends here. Small town and all." She shot back a huge smile that spread across the entire expanse of her face, and it nearly knocked him backwards. He couldn't remember the last time a simple smile had radiated so much warmth.

When they arrived back at the house, he needed to rein her in. Do this slowly, not like a herd of galloping horses. But there was no stopping her. First, she went to the ute and threw her gear in the back. Then she reached in from the passenger-side window and grabbed a soft-sided esky and flask. Then she strode purposely up the stairs and called back, "Follow me."

Follow her? Into his property? Christ, how was he going to get rid of her?

Kicking off her mud-stained boots, she left them at the door and opened the French-styled front doors without a key. Okay, so she'd done this before. She knew which direction to make for the kitchen and must've known the house was never locked.

Only a few steps behind, he forgot his earlier hesitation to enter the house; instead, he kept his gaze pinned to the small curve of her back. It wasn't enough to stop his body from flinching when he passed the wardrobe where his father used to lock him, where there was just enough space for a small boy to be crammed into the stuffy spot.

His breathing raced too fast, and he collapsed onto one of the chairs when he reached the kitchen. Was this one of the horrible memories he had to face? He kneaded his face as he tried to find some calm and stave off the lightheadedness. He'd just arrived, and already the need to leave was growing stronger than his reasons for being there.

The gurgle of water ran out of the tap for a couple of seconds before Eva turned it off. "Are you okay?"

Startled, he looked up into wary hazel-green eyes. He wasn't okay, but how did one explain how two minutes had taken him back to the seventeen-year-old boy who left this place never knowing the feeling of safety? He swallowed his annoyance at not being able to deal with this alone. It was what he wanted. Maybe to punch a few walls and tear some things down. If he decided to keep the place, he would be tearing it down anyway. What did it matter if he exorcised some demons in the process?

"O … kay," she drawled when there was no reply. "How about this question: Shall I make your tea white with sugar?"

"Sure."

She removed tin travel mugs, sugar, teabags, milk and a plastic container out of the small esky. With well-practiced precision, she laid everything out and made his cup of tea using the water from the flask.

His throat was hurting. So many goddamned tears wanted to find their way out that holding them back in front of this trespassing woman was a monumental effort. Soon the sweet aroma of the hot drink rose to meet his nose.

"Hope you like a good choc-chip biscuit. I baked them on the weekend," she said, sliding the container across the wooden kitchen table.

Whoa! How was it possible that the first food he ate in his old home was the exact favourite treat his mother used to bake for him? The memory of his father throwing a jar of them against the wall invaded his thoughts. The way they shattered into a thousand crumbs had never left him. A shiver tore across his chest.

He swallowed, doing his best not to dispel the few good memories he carried of his mother.

It was time to make a stand. "Er … Eva, thanks for this." He pointed to the tea and biscuits before asking, "Have you been inside this house before?"

She flippantly waved her hands and busied herself again making her own drink. "A couple of times."

"Recently?"

"Yeah, recently," she replied vaguely, not meeting his eyes.

He was still not happy she was trespassing but relieved she thought he was new to town. He didn't need the small community to recognise him or connect him to the monster who lived here until eight months ago. Which aged-care home his father had been moved to, he didn't care. With his father removed from the property, it was time to fulfil the promise he'd made to his mother. Even if it was the last thing he wanted to do.

She moved the biscuits closer. The baked, chocolatey smell made his traitorous stomach grumble in protest; he took one and bit into it. As delicious as it was, it scratched against his throat when he tried to swallow. He quickly took a gulp of tea. *That's better, mate. Don't rush it.*

Then Eva started rattling on about tree kangaroos, and nothing made sense. How this patch of rainforest next to his home had become an important spot in the fight against their threatened extinction. How access via his property was crucial if their fight to save the tree kangaroo was to continue. Her melodic voice, while not grating, was jarring something. Maybe it was the musty odour of the house. It hadn't changed, and the memories steamrolled through his head at an incredible speed. Until he could no longer take it.

"Look, Eva." The travel mug thumped on the kitchen table; the sound echoed around the room as Eva's voice silenced for a moment. "Thanks for the cup of tea and biscuit, but I don't think you understand." He scraped the chair back and stood. "I'm not sure what I'm going to do. I might tear it down yet and start afresh. I have my own ideas for a home, and I get you need access through this property for your tree kangaroos, but I'm not sure if I want that." Was this his final admission that he couldn't hold onto the promise he made to his mother to keep the property his grandfather had lovingly built?

Gone was the mesmerising smile Eva had shown a few times that day. Alarm stared back at him. "Are you sure? It's a solid home, about a hundred years old. Why would you want to destroy it?"

Because of all the rotten memories that nearly destroyed me, he wanted to shout back. Instead, he ground his jaw and turned away from the guilt tearing at him. He left her in the kitchen and returned to the living room with the old timber wardrobe. He stood staring at it but not really seeing it. Memories exploded behind his closed eyes like nightmares, trying to pull him back in time. He willed himself not to show any emotions, just in case Eva had followed him.

His father thought that locking him away while he dealt another blow to his mother would scare him. Yes, the dark, confined space had terrified him, but in the end, it'd had the opposite effect too.

Hidden away in the darkness was the only place he could close his mind to his mother's cries of pain and his father's harsh voice and imagine a different life. His dream to become a pilot was conceived in that darkness. In his mind, flying became the only place he could ascend above the pain and hurt, and it hadn't changed one bit. Flying was still the one place he sought solace.

He flinched at the sudden touch of Eva's hand on his shoulder.

"Sorry," she said. "I didn't mean to alarm you, and I apologise for being so blunt."

Jack turned around slowly, hoping his expression was once again neutral. She knew nothing of his past, so there was nothing to worry about.

"But how about you think on it before knocking this old place down? Spend a couple of months getting a feel for it first."

His shoulders sagged. Stay for a couple of months? She wasn't one bit sorry for being blunt. He might've taken a year off flying, but he had other business interests to consider. It was time for the big guns to come out. "Eva, I hate to be rude, but you need to leave now? I need to sort through some things."

She took a few steps back towards the door. "Sure thing." A small smile pulled at the edge of her lips. "But what are you doing tomorrow? I could use a spare pair of hands, and if you're on a break, you might enjoy the hike. I want to take some photos at the top of Windin Falls through a lensball. What do you say? It's a nine-kilometre round trip, but the view is incredible."

Oh, shit. He smiled effortlessly for the first time in what must have been ages. His face should've cracked from the sudden change. He wondered if she could talk underwater too. His smile seemed to have scared her because she took another tentative step back.

"I'll just collect my things and be gone, okay."

His smile dropped faster than heavy dew on a frosty morning. Was he giving off negative vibes? Was he his father's son? "Look, Eva, sure, I'll come with you to the falls."

She managed to compose herself again and, with a big Eva smile, said, "Great. How about I pick you up tomorrow morning at about 7 am?"

"I'm staying at The Lodge for a couple more days. The solicitor has almost finalised the settlement and I wanted a few more days to sort myself out before moving in."

"Oh, okay, that's even easier. It's on my way." With her esky zipped closed, she hugged it to her waist and made for the front door, the flask tucked under her arm. Always on the move, always in a hurry, he followed her out. She slid her muddy work boots back on and didn't worry about the laces. "See you in the morning, Jack." As she strode towards her ute, she rattled off a list of things he should take on the hike. He hoped he'd remember them because something about her left no room in his head for compiling information.

When Eva drove away, it created a weird void; it was like she was meant to stay longer. He shook his head and slid his hands into his jean pockets, strangely comforted by the overhanging rainforest surrounding the house.

Some of the tightness inside his chest lifted and drifted away as he stood in the open yard, causing his mouth to twitch at the two strange encounters he'd already experienced with this woman.

Then he remembered his reasons for coming to the house. He sighed but didn't push himself to inspect the rest of his childhood home. Yes, he needed to work through some things, but that could wait. Now that she'd left him alone, he had a compulsion to be around people.

So, he closed the front door and walked to his car. There was always tomorrow.

CHAPTER 2

Eva drove into the car park of The Lodge and spotted Jack casually leaning against the verandah post in front of his room, looking at his phone. She gave a quick toot but suspected he recognised her vehicle as soon as she drove in. There weren't too many other vehicles scrambling for attention at seven in the morning.

He picked up a backpack by his feet and headed in her direction, negating the need to park. "Good morning, Jack." She greeted cheerfully as he climbed into the ute, the familiar scent of pine filling her nostrils.

She'd made an effort to clean the ute last night, and his tall frame quickly filled up the space. Only a half-hearted "good morning" came her way, but she didn't mind. She understood more about this one person than she did about her own family. Jack's story had captivated her from the first time his father, Harold, had shared it.

She did a U-turn and drove out of the car park and onto the main road leading to Mt Bartle Frere. Constantly on the lookout for photo opportunities of the natural beauty of the north, this was one place she was familiar with since investing in the colourful *What's Up* magazine she published monthly. It catered to tourists and locals who didn't mind some adventure on their holiday or weekend.

This photo shoot and editorial would also feature in Queensland's automobile magazine, which she contributed monthly. It all paid the bills and got her into the great outdoors. Plus, it gave her the flexibility to spend time with Dr Karen and her rescued roos.

Barely giving Jack a few minutes of awkward silence, Eva knew she'd have to do the asking and most of the talking. *Okay, Jack, here goes.*

"So, wasn't it a stroke of luck you found yourself in the hardware store yesterday? You must've known Kenny was going to show up."

She peeked a quick glance at his stony straight face while waiting for traffic to pass at the Topaz Road turnoff. Recognising Jack from an old school photo Harold kept on his coffee table gave her the shock of her life.

Jack grunted, followed by, "I was told that a raincoat and a pair of gumboots are necessary if you want to live in Malanda, so I got the essentials first up. The reason I was shopping early."

Eva laughed to cover the sorrow lodged inside her chest. His reference to how wet Malanda could get wasn't a joke, but Jack was no newcomer to this town. He was a fully grown, confident, put-together man, but he wouldn't have forgotten the many hours spent in the drizzle on his four-kilometre walk to and from school each day.

"Glad that made you laugh," he said somewhat sarcastically. Before she could reply with something equally sarcastic, he asked, "What happened to the tree kangaroo you rescued?"

His concern for Kenny surprised her and touched a raw

spot inside her chest. "I took him to Dr Karen's tree rescue park."

"Is he settling in okay?"

"He is. He doesn't appear to be too traumatised, so I reckon he'll be fine. Dr Karen doesn't release the adults back into the forest, but Kenny might be one she does."

"Onto *my* property?" he grumbled under his breath.

She slammed the brakes on, veering off the bitumen and narrowly missing a school bus coming from the other direction. "Sorry about that. You can't see a damn thing around these corners. One day it'll be fatal, and then they'll widen the road."

"Here's hoping it doesn't come to that. You could always choose to drive at a snail's pace," he said, one hand gripping the dash.

"Hey! I was!" She internally fist-pumped at getting Jack to speak and merged back onto the road. Ignoring his earlier jibe about releasing roos onto his property, she steamrolled straight into her next question. "So, is there anything you want to know about tree kangaroos?" If he showed no interest like most other people, she wanted to know now; she could save herself the trouble and wasted breath from explaining.

"Where did they come from?" he asked, settling back into the seat.

"What do you mean?"

"Well, how come nobody knows much about them? You never see or read anything on them, and only because you called it a tree kangaroo did I think to look up at the trees."

Eva turned onto the rough unsealed road leading to the start of the Windin Falls walking track, and it needed all her concentration for a few moments. *Why weren't they famous?* That's the question everyone asked. She loved this furry animal so much that her life goal was to teach every Australian about the tree kangaroo's existence.

"Look, I'm sorry," Jack spluttered. "I didn't expect to arrive at my property and find it overrun with rescued tree kangaroos and someone waltzing inside my home like they lived there."

Once she'd navigated a large pothole and a boulder jutting onto the track, Eva's shoulders sagged. She remembered Harold telling her that Jack would be untrusting and resentful. *And* Jack spoke the truth. She knew the house very well. She'd helped Harold clean it up and removed his personal effects and any traces of a boy who once lived there. 'If I take away the reminders, it'll help him heal,' Harold had said.

"I apologise too, Jack. The plan was to discuss the roo rescue plan with you when you arrived. We are only a couple of days late, aren't we?"

Jack harrumphed.

When he didn't say anything else, she barrelled straight in. "Did you know the Lumholtz tree kangaroo is found nowhere else in the world? Can you believe that?"

"It's not the first animal unique to an area." He continued to stare out the front windscreen.

"But it makes it special to *our* local area. Except everything is going against them, and I don't want this generation responsible for their extinction."

Jack sighed, and a quick peek in his direction showed he'd closed his eyes for a moment. *Frustrated? Bored? Tired?* Gritting her teeth, she braced for his retort.

"Okay, the damn things can stay on the property until I get sorted. But I make no promises about it being some sort of long-term roo resort."

A bubble of laughter unexpectedly escaped Eva's mouth.

It wasn't the retort she was expecting. It was beyond anything she expected. His property bordered Dr Karen's, and to shift her precious roos because a landowner wanted them off their property wasn't a decision she was prepared to confront yet. So, she turned the volume up on the radio and tapped the steering wheel in time to the song playing, even singing a line or two she knew.

"Why are you so happy?" He asked grumpily.

"Because, Jack, you've just made my day." She veered off the road and onto a cleared patch of grass marked for vehicle parking and stopped. "See, I told you. Good fresh air and already your mind is uncluttering."

Jack shook his head and opened his door. He probably rolled his eyes too. "I haven't promised anything, Eva."

"You don't have to, Jack. Not yet anyway. Now, let's get some good photos of this view. It'll blow you away."

She pulled on the hand brake and reached behind the seat in the dual cab for her backpack. If she wasn't mistaken, she was sure she'd just witnessed a small smile tug at the edges of his mouth. He was human, after all.

After learning the sad story of his childhood, it'd been her greatest fear that when Jack returned to reclaim his property, he would be an unfeeling chunk of wood, putting the roos they worked so hard to protect at risk.

Unexpected joy buzzed throughout her body. *I think I might've got it all wrong.*

Eva strode a few steps ahead of him, embarrassingly showing Jack up. A few weeks of laziness and the slight incline left him puffing and his chest aching. A stickler for regularly doing his gym sessions, since deciding to take a year off work and returning to the north, he'd fallen into a despondent hole with little motivation.

He took some long strides and fell in beside her. "How long have you lived up here?" he puffed.

She turned a surprised face in his direction.

Yes, I can be sociable if I try.

She slowed her step and shortened her stride. For her height, she walked fast. "I was born on the Tablelands. After my mother died when I was three, Dad took my sister and me back to Brisbane to be closer to Nan and Pop. They helped him a lot with raising us."

"And you came back, when?"

"Five years ago. The opportunity came up to buy the rights to produce a local magazine, and I took it."

Jack nodded. *No screwed-up life in any of that.* "What's it about?"

"Do you want to have a ten-minute break and I'll explain?"

They stopped at the top of a small crest, and he linked his hands behind his head, straightened and sucked in a few deep breaths. He wasn't this unfit, was he? "How much longer is there to go?"

"About another two k's."

"Yeah, a break will be great. I didn't think a few weeks of no exercise would leave me feeling so haggard. If anything, I was certain my height would've given me the advantage."

Eva's laughter tinkled into the crisp morning air. The forest wasn't so thick where they stood, and the morning sun rested golden hues across her flushed face. "I might be short, but I've always been a fast walker."

Touché. Inhaling the heady and rich smell of the earth and its trees, something wholesome tugged inside his chest. How did he get here? After wanting to return to his old home and hide away like a hermit, he'd come across more people in the last twenty-four hours than during the previous month of planning this trip. Encountering this woman for the third time in such a short time had to be a record.

When she stopped laughing and looked across at him, he could've sworn a flicker of something like worry crossed her face. Why would she care about him? He was a stranger who had newly arrived in town. Usually, he received looks of appreciation from women he didn't know. He wasn't unaware of the good looks he inherited from his monster of a father. He'd been told often enough but avoided thinking about their shared traits.

Her frown morphed into a mischievous smile. "If you're interested, I have six months' worth of hiking to do. You're welcome to join me any time. You'll be fit before you know it."

This trip to the north would be well and truly finished by then, but he didn't tell her that.

Sitting on a large protruding rock under the loose canopy of forest trees, she opened her backpack and pulled out a Kit Kat, tearing the wrapping open. "Here, take half."

With a famous sweet tooth, Jack didn't argue. With an extra helping of sugar and a good drink of water, he sat on a smaller rock and rested his legs. "So, what's this magazine of yours all about?"

Scrunching up the Kit Kat wrapper and putting it in her bag, she slid down the rock closer to where he sat. It might've been his imagination, but a sudden heat flared between them, and he leant away.

"It's called *What's Up*. It's glossy and bright and showcases community events and festivals on the Tablelands. I make my money from the adverts. It also features hiking trips that families and tourists can do. I walk them all first, so

I can tell them firsthand what's needed and how long it'll take, whether small children can handle it and that sort of thing. I also cover bike trails because the Tablelands is becoming quite famous for it."

"Just like its tree roos?" Jack quirked an eyebrow in her direction.

Again, her laughter echoed around the narrow track and surrounded him comfortably. "Jack, you're catching on quick."

Her words put him in a good place. He'd do anything to see another one of her smiles though. When she did everything else disappeared into insignificance. It blinded him like nothing before had, leaving him floundering for anything sensible to say.

But it was time to move his sorry, lazy arse and get back on the track. He rose and stretched his legs. "Okay, taskmaster, lead the way. We're not there yet."

For that remark, she awarded him another brilliant smile, enabling him to forget about his lack of fitness.

CHAPTER 3

Thank God Jack cleaned his act up and got over his case of grumps, Eva mused as she set the pace for the final two kilometres. Anyone who accompanied her on her hikes had to be keen and not linger too far behind. Groaners and whingers were syphoned off her list of volunteers, whether they wanted to be or not. This was probably why the list was relatively short.

When she found Jack waiting that morning for *her,* and not the other way round, he'd earned his first tick. When he roused himself for the final two k's, sounding keen to get going, he scored a second tick. If he gasped with wonder at the amazing view that never ceased to amaze her, she'd award him his third tick. So far, so good.

"What do you do for a job, Jack?"

He groaned. She ignored it. He may as well get used to it. She would never shut up.

"I'm a pilot."

Oh. She turned her head to look at him better. This knowledge lent a new light to everything. Not even Harold knew what his son did for a living.

"For Qantas, in case you were about to ask." He threw her a sideways glance before focusing on the uneven track.

She was, but she chuckled instead. Could he read her so well?

"Domestic and International, if this is your next question."

Eva raised her hands in defence. "Hey, don't let me stop you from talking. I'm happy to say nothing for the rest of the day."

"I'd have to see that to believe it."

Wow. She had him smiling again, and what a sight to behold, even if it was lopsided and … maybe bashful. Somehow, he'd tied her tongue in knots. She might never talk again.

"We must be close now?" he eventually asked.

She nodded and pointed to a change in direction. "This is the final stretch. Try not to walk over the edge; there's no fencing and only some boulders to protect it. There's also an infinity pool you can sit in if the current isn't too strong."

"Can you see the actual waterfall?"

Patting her trusty backpack, she said, "Not without my drone."

"What will we see?"

"Wait a few minutes, and then tell me it wasn't worth getting up early for."

Climbing over the last of the boulders and back into the sunshine, Eva kept her gaze on Jack's face without making it too obvious. She didn't know why it was so important he appreciated something that always left her mouth hanging open, no matter how many times she ventured this way.

At the top, she pointed to a large boulder. "This is the one you don't walk past, or you'll fling yourself out into the never-never."

Jack stood stock-still, the view working its magic over him as she hoped. A person only reacted this way when the view had an effect on them. She understood it because it happened to her every time.

Shrugging off his backpack, he ventured closer, laying on his stomach to look over the edge. All the more daring hikers did that. Well, the more daring humans in the herd anyway.

"So, what do you think?" she asked, doing her best to ignore the image he presented as he spread himself over the cliff face.

Jack shook his head. "I know a lot about the north, but I never knew this place existed." Was that regret in his voice? Growing up, had no one brought him up here? Come to think of it, few people ventured this way. It was a relatively new waterfall on the circuit of things to do on the Tablelands but was quickly gaining popularity.

As she set out a small picnic on a patch of grass, she let him savour the view and gorge on the stunning sight of rainforest-covered mountains crisscrossing into the distant horizon for as far as the eye could see. In the morning shade, the contours were better visible, hence the early start.

The wind would spray back a water mist over your face as the falls cascaded over the top. The thundering sound of rushing water less than a metre beside you, as it tumbled over into the massive void, always left a tingle of sensation along her skin. Once she set the drone into flight, the image of the falls would blow him away.

Already satisfied with his reaction, she ticked box number three. Once he saw the actual falls, she'd be scrambling to tick box number four. This made her heart soar.

Switching her mind off the glorious view of Jack's backside in comfortably fitted hiking pants was hard work for her brain in its current man-drought. She sighed and pulled her gaze back to the equipment in hand. She had to get her shots in early before the sun rose too high or other hikers arrived and invaded her screen space.

"Okay, Jack, I need to get this show on the road. Have a quick snack, and then I could use some help."

Jack shimmied back from the edge before standing and turning around, looking surprised at the banquet she'd spread. "How did you manage all this within the space of minutes?"

"Lots of practice. Come on, eat up. I didn't bring all this food to carry it back."

"I should've carried it. You have the camera and drone as well." A forlorn look crossed his face, and it was kind of adorable.

"Nah, I think you were struggling enough." She smirked.

"What?" And they both burst out laughing. Eva couldn't believe how much ribbing she was getting away with. Cautious with what she knew about his past, she was excited she could get him to relax around her. That was another promise she'd made to Harold.

Jack's stomach grumbled so loud it could've echoed around the valley. For a few weeks there, food hadn't rated high on his list of priorities.

Eva had a ham and salad wrap waiting for him, some sliced cheese and crackers, fresh fruit already peeled and sliced, and a small tub of yoghurt. The sweet smell of the fruit reached him first, so he started with half a mango that he turned inside out, eating the flesh from the skin.

"Thanks, this will hit the spot. It's a lot healthier than what I usually eat, but it's exactly what I needed after that power walk up the hill."

She smiled that brilliant Eva smile, and his stomach flipped stupidly.

"It's a con. I lure you with food and then expect you to work hard. Think you can handle it?"

Jack swallowed roughly and gazed at her. Her smile slipped momentarily before she looked past him, back across the valley.

"Don't you get many offers of help?" he asked.

She picked up a cracker and a slice of cheese. "I get too many. I'm still searching for the best volunteer in the world. I have strict criteria."

Her smile was back in place, but something happened just there, and his heart lurched, skipping a couple of beats. It wasn't like he was going to win any awards. As soon as she understood his intentions for the property were nothing like she hoped, he'd fall to the bottom of her list. There wouldn't be too many more offers to accompany her on the hikes, and that would be a shame.

"What do I need to do to remain at the top?"

Her gaze was intense and searching as she watched him closely and moved to pack away the empty containers and neatly stowed them in her backpack. "Can you hold a lensball?"

"I reckon I can."

"Good, that should just about do it. Here, catch."

Without a moment to spare, a round, clear ball came his way, and it fell into his lap. He held it up to the morning light and realised it wasn't clear. "Hmm, interesting." He'd never seen one used before and was curious about how it worked.

Eva pushed her backpack aside and fiddled with her camera. A lot of photography paraphernalia had come out of her bag, and the drone was yet to make its appearance. "Stand over here and hold the lensball at about this height."

He stood and followed Eve's instructions. She touched his hand which held the ball and guided it to her desired height. Something tingled along his skin, and her clean, crisp scent played havoc with his senses. His gaze skirted towards hers and an unusual expression flickered across her face. For some weird reason, he kept seeing it as sympathy. Or did she feel something too and this was her way of showing it?

Neither moved for a breath until he dropped his face and let her get on with the job. If he was finding it hard to breathe, that was his problem. *Let her get the photos.*

When she'd taken all the photos she needed with the lensball, she handed him the camera to view the images on the back screen. He crouched down and leant against a rock. The photos awed him. "Wow," He muttered. A second image was captured upside down in the ball's sphere while the real one surrounded it. How had he never seen something so simple but amazing? As he swiped through the photos, each one had him holding his breath as though she had created some magic.

The noise of the drone whirring as it rose from the ground sounded loud in the pristine quiet at the top of the world. It was one of those rare feelings where it felt like you were the only two humans in the world and standing at some gateway. Surely nothing bad happened when you could look out at this amazing view with an equally interesting woman.

Jack swallowed, his throat suddenly dry. Where had those thoughts come from? He wrinkled his nose and gently cradled the camera on his lap as Eva expertly sent the drone into the air. Why couldn't he take his eyes off her? And why was there a ridiculous smile on his face? Questions and more questions and not a single answer for any of them.

Of one thing he was certain. He needed to sort himself out.

CHAPTER 4

"Did you wear your swimmers?" Eva asked as she twisted the lens from the camera body and placed it in a padded bag.

"I did, but isn't it a bit cold?" A brisk morning breeze licked at his face, and he couldn't imagine stripping down and plunging into the icy water.

"Always chilly when you first get in, but I'm not letting you leave without having swum in the infinity pool. And we haven't got all day."

Jack raised his eyebrows and chuckled at her bluntness. Anyone else ordering him around would've got a scowl, but something about Eva's enthusiasm didn't allow that.

When he looked up from untying his bootlace, she quickly pulled her eyes away. He didn't miss the slight blush creeping up her neck. Did she think she'd overstepped the mark? "Am I safe?" he asked.

Eva laughed, cheeky and teasing. "Only someone who deliberately hurts my roos isn't safe around me." Then she looked from left to right. "And I can't see anyone here who might toss you over the edge."

Jack managed a crooked smile, realising she

misinterpreted his question. If he was getting a vibe, it was Eva's obsession with protecting the tree kangaroo. As he unbuttoned his shirt, he recalled the promise he'd made to his mum. In the years since, it'd slowly slipped into the background. Was he going to get caught up in a storm with a bunch of furry animals in the middle of it?

Don't ever forget that I love you, Jack. Take this bank book and use it to get your dream. You deserve it. And when you come back, the house will be yours and only yours. Do what you need to do to take away the bad memories but promise me you'll keep it. Your grandfather intended it as a happy place to raise a family. I'm sorry I couldn't do that …

Jack promised his mother he would, and it had sat on his conscience all these years. But so much had happened in the time that had passed. He didn't need the property anymore. After overhearing two businessmen talk at a café where he worked his first job, a chance gamble on the stock market had set off a chain reaction of solid investments and a string of high-end properties. His life in the fast lane was a world away from his sad childhood.

With his shirt off and his mind in a muddle, he'd just unbuttoned his hiking pants when a white tube was thrust in his face. He jolted at the intrusion.

"Here, put some sunscreen on. I forgot to mention to bring your own."

As Jack reached for it, his pants fell to his ankles. But he'd forgotten to take his boots off, and Eva burst out laughing at the comical sight. A deep sound came from his stomach and bubbled from his throat.

As he leant against the tree for balance and kicked off his boots, it hit him. He'd laughed more in the past twenty-four hours with Eva than he had in a lifetime. Recalling his mother's last words hadn't tormented him like usual. What was it with this woman? It felt good, and he'd be damned if he would shy away and not look at her.

She undressed to reveal a toned body clad in a black one-piece swimsuit. Her petite frame was more muscular than he expected, clearly fit and healthy. Yeah, a long way from the women he usually dated. Mostly, they were tall, slim and expensively dressed. Curiously, his body stirred in reaction to what was in front of him.

"Sunscreen, Jack," she said, breaking into his ruminations.

At her reminder, he dropped his gaze and didn't care that she'd caught him ogling. He hadn't expected the memory of his mother thrusting an old and battered savings book at him to coincide with Eva doing a similar thing with the sunscreen. Even though it brought back a flood of memories, today, he would enjoy a refreshing swim with a woman fate had thrust in his path.

Eva was already waist deep when he decided he'd done tougher and more daring stuff over the years. With sunscreen on, it was time to man up. Except, he was savouring the warm sun and didn't relish the thought of ice-cold water rushing over his skin.

"It's not deep, so you're going to have to drop your knees. Come over this way and sit on these rocks that act as a ledge."

"Bloody hell." Jack sucked in a breath when the cool water iced up around his legs. "Is this some torture test to sort out the volunteers who are stayers or goers?"

Eva's head tipped back as she laughed again, despite his remark being serious. Her laughter was having a strange effect on him again. In desperation to get the ordeal over and done with, he dropped his knees, hollered out into the void and pummelled his chest like Tarzan until his body temperature adjusted.

Bending over with laughter, she tugged on his arm and guided him to the cool and slippery rocks beside her. "Better not tempt fate and stay in the current that's pushing the water over the top."

Over the top? Jack settled in beside Eva. Close enough for their shoulders to touch in the confined space of the infinity pool. Then it dawned on him what they were doing. They were sitting within a metre of the top of a waterfall, with water flowing past them and over the cliff. This was no enclosed space. This was no wardrobe where he was locked inside. It was like flying. He was soaring. He was free, and when he turned to Eva, her eyes were full of questions and sympathy and something that looked a little like … lust. Were his emotions showing on his face? Was the desire to kiss her obvious? If it was, it was too late to hide. He trailed a finger down her cheek, cupped her face and drew her closer until their lips met. From her warm mouth to his, nothing was cold anymore.

Eva anchored herself to his solid shoulder. For a moment, she was terrified she'd be carried by the current and swept away, so she squeezed her fingers harder, not wanting the moment to end. Still, his firm mouth remained attached to hers, tongue seeking, sweeping, probing, warming her from the inside. She wasn't going anywhere. Not when everything in the world felt right for once.

When Jack pulled away, a look of concern stared back at her, like he'd done a terrible thing. Her chest ached, and she desperately wanted him back. When he spoke, it confirmed her fears.

"Oh, my God, Eva, I'm so sorry. I shouldn't have done that." A wave sloshed over the pool as he stood and scrambled over the rocks to get out.

"No, wait, Jack." Hadn't she promised Harold she'd take good care of him? She followed him out and wrapped a towel around herself.

"Bloody hell, I've known you one day. That was wrong. I need to control myself better."

But for Eva, who'd lived through Harold's stories, it felt like she'd known him forever, and the pull to tell him nearly brought her undone. The constant reminder that she didn't have forever left was pushed firmly to the back of her mind. She wouldn't let the anxiety that had plagued her for most of her life find a cushy place in her head that day.

Jack hastily wrapped his towel around his torso, and together they dried and dressed in silence. Eva knew she had to say something to break the unnecessary awkwardness. If anything, she wanted to demand he kiss her again. What did he think was wrong with a gorgeous man wanting to kiss her? Unless it'd been distasteful to him. This was enough to wipe every vestige of talk right out of her.

With Jack dressed and ready to leave, he clambered onto a large boulder and took in the view of the valley. She gave him space, some time to stew in his thoughts. Well, for a couple of minutes while she packed away the camera and drone. She didn't want to end the morning like this and have to walk all the way back in uncomfortable silence. So, she did the most annoying thing she could think of. She climbed right up beside him on the boulder that could barely fit two people.

Jack sighed heavily. "What are you doing, Eva?"

He flicked his gaze upwards as though searching for a

bird or plane, but he was obviously trying to avoid looking at her. She inched closer, annoyingly putting herself in his space. "Sitting beside you."

He huffed and shuffled over a few centimetres. "Why?"

Jack had no choice but to grab her by the arm before they both toppled off. "I don't want to leave it like this. This view is too special to leave with a bad taste in my mouth."

"So, my kiss was in bad taste, or was there a bad taste in my mouth?"

"No," she wailed into the valley, and it echoed back. She clung to Jack's shirt and tried but failed horribly at not laughing when it was apparent Jack was not in the laughing mood.

He was scowling, and it didn't appear she was succeeding in her plan to end this hike on a cheerful note. "Kiss me again, Jack."

"What are you going on about?" His frown deepened.

"Kiss me again, and I promise not to talk the whole walk back." She fluttered her eyelashes for good luck.

Clinging to each other, he cocked a brow in her direction and shook his head. She almost lost her position as she drowned in his blue eyes. She swallowed and chewed on the inside of her lip. *Her* smile had long gone. What if he refused to?

"I don't believe you. You'll have to promise me something else," he said straight-faced.

She scrambled for something else. Anything so he'd kiss her. He was right. She'd never keep her mouth shut for the walk back. She licked her suddenly dry lips, determined she wanted his mouth to moisten them. "Ah … okay, I promise to show you around the roo rescue park and teach you everything I know about why the tree kangaroo is so important to me."

Jack groaned, and the echo reverberated around the valley.

"Hey, that's gold in my books," she protested.

"I'm not groaning about that." He sighed, resigned, and moved his arms to grip her around the waist. "It's been twenty-four hours, three encounters and one kiss. We barely know each other and you want to add another kiss to it?"

"Yes," she said on a breathy note.

A pulse ticked beneath the skin on his temple. His breath hitched, and he groaned one last time before his face dropped enough for his mouth to touch hers. Heat flared from within her breasts the longer the kiss continued. She was getting her money's worth. When his tongue slid in and touched hers, she moaned quietly, convinced she'd float out into the void to be lost forever. It wouldn't be such a bad way to go.

A warning twigged inside her head, and she tried to push it away. Ignoring it, she willed the kiss to go on and on, not wanting it to end. With every nerve ending tingling over her body, stars burst behind her closed eyes. If she dizzily fell off this rock, it wouldn't be her fault. But a niggle that she was yet to tell Jack everything she knew wouldn't go away. God help her. How could she bring his father into the conversation? Or tell him about the curse. He'd run a mile and hate her in the process.

With great reluctance, she pulled back and took big, gulping breaths. At that exact moment, voices approached the top of the falls. *Good.* She could use their arrival as her excuse. When Jack learnt how much she knew about him and the fear she lived with every day, she'd be responsible for this brooding and serious man to drop further into the sinkhole. She'd stepped over a line, and kissing him compounded the problem. Enjoying it and wanting more would be her eventual ruin.

She slid down the boulder and landed with a thump on the ground. "Time to go, Jack." She got up and rubbed her backside where she landed on a couple of sharp rocks.

Jack slid off with reluctance, his gaze burning a hole right through her as they stared at each other. The arrival of several backpackers broke the awkward silence. They exchanged smiles and all ventured a hello in their various accents. Eva chatted for a few moments, asking where they were from and played the well-worn role of the welcoming local.

Jack didn't utter a word, just stood to the side, hands in his pockets. After all, he wasn't a local, and if she sufficiently pissed him off, it wouldn't take much for him to sell his property and leave. There were no good memories there.

She couldn't afford to make an offer on it, but someone else would. Driven by what was important to her, she would do everything to make Jack want to stay. She would ensure the property remained largely as it was with the abundant rainforest undisturbed to permanently house the roos in her care. And, damn it, she wanted Jack to kiss her again.

Ah … yup. The complications just compounded, and a tiny pulse pounded against her temple.

She tipped her head in Jack's direction when the backpackers lost interest, the view becoming their priority. "Ready?"

He gave a slight nod and bent to retrieve his backpack. Believe it or not, she didn't utter a single word the entire walk back. Unsurprisingly, neither did Jack. Until they climbed into the vehicle, and Jack uttered the last words she expected to hear.

"You owe me a tour of the roo rescue park."

She turned to face him, sure her jaw was sitting on her lap. Like a mechanical robot, she closed it with slow, jerky movements. "Okay, how about Tuesday?" She had to work this carefully and make sure it wasn't the day Harold and the bunch of oldies she gathered from the aged-care facility volunteered at the park.

If everything Harold had told her was true, then Jack wasn't ready for that confrontation.

CHAPTER 5

The Lodge wasn't the usual place Jack stayed, but Malanda had limited choices. The silence was unnerving. The sound of his thoughts couldn't dispel it. For some reason, he craved chatter. The kind that only Eva could provide. Spending so much time with her that morning made it harder for Jack to find solace in being alone.

He swung his legs over the edge of the bed and raked a hand through his dishevelled hair. Eva. Of all the braindead things to do, he'd made the first move and kissed her. Shaking his head, he plugged in the kettle and flicked it on. Why did he do something so stupid? Twenty-four fucking hours. Who was he? The last thing he needed was to create a connection with this place. He wanted to carry through with his plans and get the hell back to his life—the one he'd created with hard work and sensible investment decisions.

When he located a mug in the cupboard, he tore open a coffee sachet from the welcome freebies and emptied the contents into it. That she was as rattled as he'd been was evident by how she hadn't spoken a single word on the walk back. It had torn at him. He wanted the chattering Eva. He wanted her to talk about anything and everything. It didn't matter what, providing her soothing voice washed over him. Instead, he'd been tense the entire way back and had no one to blame but himself.

Then agreeing to kiss her a second time. He forgot about his coffee and flopped back on the bed. Rolling onto his stomach, he scrunched the crisp cotton pillow against his face and groaned like a caveman. It'd been fucking unbelievable the second time, and his betraying body, even now, was showing the obvious sign of how much he enjoyed it.

When the kettle boiled and switched off, he made another attempt to get up. It was time to confront the real world again and get through the rest of Sunday and Monday. Stupidly, Tuesday was his next goal. He'd clung onto anything to make sure he saw her again and blurted out a reminder of her promise without thinking.

Pouring the boiled water into his mug, he chuckled unexpectedly. In the quiet room, it almost alarmed him. That he could laugh and smile when his morose thoughts would usually dig in deeper. He made a snap decision. He would check-out a day early and attempt to move temporarily into his childhood home. Regardless of the promise he'd made to his mother, he had to know if he could handle being there.

"Bloody hell!" Jack arrived at the property to find the familiar white ute parked in his drive. How often did she drop by to check on her roos?

"Eva!" This had to stop. This was his place, and she had to at least get his permission to enter it. When there was no response, he rushed to the front door, pulling it open. "Eva?" he called out again, not so aggressively this time.

Turning on the spot, he knew exactly where she would be. Whether he could find his way back to the collection of tree kangaroos, he wasn't so sure.

Eva burst out of the rainforest as he made his way to the back of the property.

Her eyes widened when they landed on him. "Hey, Jack. I didn't expect to see you here so soon." Her sunny smile radiated back at him, but it wasn't enough to curb the roiling anger in his stomach.

"Why?" he asked curtly. Damn it, while he had initially craved Eva's chatter, he didn't want a stampede crossing his property whenever she chose.

She stopped short and dropped her backpack to the ground. "Hey, look, I'm sorry. I should ask for your permission first, shouldn't I?"

The roiling anger in his stomach changed to nervous anxiety. An awful suspicion was building down there, but he pushed it aside. *Not possible.* It must've been an arrangement with the friendly solicitor. It wasn't like he would ask if she knew his father. His father didn't make friends.

The bubbly and energetic woman from the morning's hike was gone. A worried frown replaced her sunny smile. He cursed under his breath and ploughed a hand through his hair. For most of the afternoon, he'd been mooning about wanting to kiss her again. It wasn't going to happen this way. "Look, Eva, I'm sorry. I didn't mean it like that. This"—he motioned his arms to the rainforest—"has caught me off guard. I wasn't expecting to share my property with a bunch of furry animals and someone so dedicated to them." He let out a frustrated sigh. "How did the previous resident deal with this?"

In an instant, her sunny smile was back. "We rarely saw him, but we had permission to use the property for access. He mostly kept to himself."

He inwardly groaned. It would take some work to get rid of her … if this was his intention. But for now, he could relax a little, knowing she had no idea it was his father they spoke of.

Eva pulled her phone out of her back pocket and swiped it once. "Do you have some spare time now?"

He rolled back on his heels and shoved his hands in his pockets. "I'm moving into the house a couple of days earlier. I was going to unpack my swag and gear. I don't have much else with me. Some basic stuff will arrive early next week."

"I tell you what. I'll help you do it later. How about you follow me, and I'll show you how amazing the position of your property is? It's about a half-k walk." She pulled out a roll of something bright pink from another pocket and held it up. "Some trusty flagging tape and you'll be able to do this on your own."

Jack frowned, not even close to understanding what she was blabbering about. "Wait." He took a step forward and reached for her shoulder. Before she turned towards the rainforest again, he asked, "Where are we going?"

She chuckled, and it soothed him. "I should explain, shouldn't I?"

He nodded slowly, unable to tear his gaze away. His hand remained resting on her shoulder, and when the warmth radiated between them, he let it drop and shuffled back. Eva chewed her bottom lip, looking uncertain for a change. This was unlike the Eva who he was fast getting used to with her 'foot down and hurtling' approach to everything.

Anxiety twisted in his gut when she sighed and her shoulders dropped dejectedly. "Your property borders on the southern side of the roo rescue park that Dr Karen and her husband own. That's why this patch of rainforest is so important. The more rainforest we have, the more tree roos we can rescue and release into a safe space."

So this was why Eva and her band of volunteers wanted to continue as usual. His appearance on the scene put a spanner in the works. Their alarm that he would demand no one enter his property was real, going by the worried look on Eva's face. What had the solicitor told them? Did they already know he was the son of the bastard living here before? He wasn't about to enlighten them. The less he shared about his past, the better. He'd be gone from this place as fast as possible, but the last thing he wanted to do was upset Eva.

Gritting his teeth, he inwardly swore again. "Okay, show me," he volunteered. *I may as well get the ordeal over and done with.* When she presented another brilliant smile, his chest expanded so much that he managed a half-smile in response.

"That's better, Jack. A smile suits you," Eva stated, turning back to the forest.

"What?" Already he'd replaced it with a scowl she couldn't see.

Her laughter drifted back to him, and the chill of the canopied forest as they entered it cooled his thoughts. He gulped in a lungful of rainforest air and exhaled slowly. *Get it together, mate.* Unconsciously, he rubbed his arm as goosebumps appeared; at the same time, Eva tore short lengths off the flagging tape and tied it around trees in their path. "You'll have to stay quiet if you want to see my babies again."

He didn't mean for the groan to sound so loud when it escaped his mouth.

"That's not quiet, Jack," she flung back over her shoulder. He caught a glimpse of her hazel-green eyes when a thin ray of sunlight squeezed through the thick canopy. They sparkled for a split second before she turned away again. He swallowed back a sense of loss of not being able to hold them longer.

Stop it, idiot. When he least expected it or felt like it, when he wanted to climb into his black hole and stay there forever, Eva had a way of dragging him into unknown territory, quite literally.

What he would find at the connecting border, he had no idea. But something about Eva had him following her like a loyal pet *and* with a bounce in his step.

These were strange times.

One step behind, Jack followed Eva as she marked a clear trail with the bright pink flagging tape. Her sure-footed direction didn't falter once, leading Jack to believe she'd walked this route a few times before. Every three or four metres, she swiftly tied a piece of flagging tape around a branch. There'd be no chance he'd get lost if he ventured on this walk alone. Now he understood what she was doing.

He recognised the spot from the previous day, and his gaze drifted up to the many tree kangaroos congregated in the rainforest's canopy.

Hearing a shuffle beside him, he looked back to find Eva pulling a small yoga-styled mat out of her backpack and spreading it out beside a tree. "It's hard to come here and not spend a few minutes. Come and sit on the mat. It might prevent the leeches from crawling up and finding a warm spot on you."

Now leeches *were* something he remembered from his childhood. Nasty little bloodsucking creatures!

They sat, not quite back-to-back, but on an angle, their shoulders touching. A spot that instantly warmed. Jack tried to ignore it and leant against the soft lichen on the tree. He closed his eyes and raised his face, letting the peaceful sound of bird chatter fill the surrounding space. One day he'd learn more about them.

If there was one decent memory to gather from his childhood, it was the potent smell of the forest. He sucked in a deep breath and released it evenly through his lips. Honestly, a mere week ago, he would've never imagined he would be doing this. He'd envisioned so much anguish and suppressed anger bubbling to the surface upon his arrival. Then again, he hadn't spent any time in the house yet. That was where the horrors had occurred.

"It's relaxing, isn't it?" she whispered. "It always helps me after a rushed deadline when my brain is buzzing at a hundred miles an hour."

Jack gently butted her shoulder and opened his eyes. "Shush. You told me we had to be quiet."

She butted his shoulder back. "I am being quiet … for me."

Jack focused on a cheeky roo scurrying along a branch and muffled a groan. He did his best to rein the noise, but he couldn't hold back the smile that twitched at his mouth. She *was* being quiet for Eva, he got that much, but he hadn't been able to help himself with the retort.

When more soft sounds and shaky movements came from Eva, he slid around on his backside to double-check if his suspicions were correct. With her hand covering her mouth and doing her best to stifle the sound, she struggled to contain her belly laugh. It was hard not to succumb, and they fell into fits of laughter like a couple of schoolchildren. The type of laughter that got every muscle in the chest and stomach to move, leaving you full of feel-good endorphins and tears streaming down your cheeks. They might've startled some roos because there was shuffling in the canopy and a gentle thud on the forest floor as they hopped away.

Somewhere in all the amusement, their foreheads touched; his hand found her hip, and his lips briefly pressed hers. When that happened, the laughter stopped, and his gaze collided with hers. It was intense like she was trying to read him, to make sense of his actions and manner. She was just as intriguing. What was going through her mind? Unable to endure the scrutiny, he shuffled back on the mat and returned his attention to the roos.

"I guess we should keep going?" Eva whispered.

"I guess so."

They stood and Jack rolled the mat up, shoved it into her backpack, and slung it over his shoulder. When she didn't immediately move, he spotted that weird look of concern or pity on her face again. He physically turned her around and gave her a gentle nudge to indicate she should start walking, all the while shaking his head and not understanding a thing. But the niggle wouldn't go away.

CHAPTER 6

Eva stopped at a fallen tree that blocked the narrow path, and the crunch of Jack's steps came to a halt behind her. "Ever done mountain bike riding?" she asked before turning around in the narrow space.

Jack took a step back, the backpack dangling at his side. Eva swallowed roughly, still finding it hard to believe how incredibly good-looking he was. His broodiness and gruffness didn't detract from it at all. If anything, it added an air of mystery and intrigue. She'd kept up a continuous conversation, doing everything to keep her mind off how his closeness affected her and tried her darndest to push the memory of that brief kiss to the back of her head.

"No. With my flying, I'm rarely in one place for long."

"Where's home?" she asked, leaning against what was left of an old fence post.

"Brisbane."

Eva nodded as she casually twisted the remnants of a rusted piece of barbed wire. She was used to his one- or two-word replies. She'd barrelled along the borderline between the two properties, doing most of the talking and pointing out fascinating plants and animals. The four hundred metre walk had taken longer than necessary, but they were lucky to see a leaf-tailed gecko, a golden orb spider, a green tree frog perched on a small sapling and an azure kingfisher staring down at them from a thick branch.

She used her phone to snap photos of everything, always exhilarated at the prospect of using them as fillers in her glossy magazine. The one shot she took of Jack looking up at the green tree frog was already a favourite. She tried not to grin as she expanded the image on the screen again. She hoped she didn't waste precious sleeping hours looking at it later. If Jack agreed, she'd use it in her next edition.

"What's funny?"

Her head snapped up. It wasn't unusual to be lost in her thoughts when alone, but with company—. Instead of feeling mortified at where her mind had gone, she slipped the phone into her back pocket with a loud guffaw. Some forest floor dwellers scampered through the undergrowth, scampering away from her sudden outburst. "I could tell you, but then I'd have to kill you."

She scored a good roll of the eyes for that one. *Oh, man.* Jack needed some lessons on chilling out and when to smile.

"Okay, not so funny then?" She asked. This elicited a reluctant smile from him.

"That's better, Jack." Another scowl. What had she taken on when she'd promised Harold to take care of him? "I'm trialling a new bike track with the club tomorrow and featuring it in next month's edition. You want to come?"

Jack scratched his dark hair, a confused expression crossing his face. "Won't I need a bike and helmet?"

"Of course. I'll let the bike rental company know there'll be two of us. By the way," she said, pointing to the post, "this is where your boundary ends." She rested her hand on the old fence post and let him process it.

He looked left and then right, but it wouldn't have mattered. Other than the stringy-bark post and the rusted barbed wire, there was nothing else to separate the two properties.

"The rescue park is another hundred metres. You're welcome to come any time. We always appreciate volunteers." She made the offer, despite concern about the possibility of Jack confronting his father there. Would Jack be the type to volunteer? She wasn't sure she had anything to worry about.

When he didn't add anything further to the conversation, she pointed to the track and started walking. "Let's get this show on the road as there are never enough hours in the day."

"Do you ever sleep?"

She stopped and spun around. "What do you mean?"

With the backpack secured on his back, he folded his arms and uncomfortably scrutinised her, like he was trying to work her out. *Good luck with that, mate.* "You fit in a thousand things a day. You volunteer at this place, you rescue tree kangaroos on other days, you publish your own tourist magazine, and what did you say you also did, about the monthly automobile club magazine—"

"Yeah, I contribute some of my stories from *What's Up* each month."

"This is my point. When do you take timeout?"

She put on her bravest smile, doing everything possible to combat the thought that someone had caught her out for the very first time. She swallowed back painful emotions that always struck her when she thought about her predicament and the curse. "Everything I do is timeout because I love it." She straightened and squared her shoulders. "What if you died tomorrow, Jack? Would you be satisfied you'd lived life to the fullest? If your days were numbered, wouldn't you want to fit in as much as possible?"

He tipped his head to the side and frowned at her statement. "What are you talking about? I need a decent rest, but I don't think about dying. Not yet anyway."

She shrugged. There was no point trying to get him to understand. It was time to shut the conversation down before it left her a wreck. "Six in the morning if you want to come."

He nodded slowly. "Can I pick you up this time?"

She hadn't missed his luxurious LandCruiser. "Nah, I'll need my ute to transport the bikes." *Still, it would've been nice to experience a ride in it.*

"Oh, okay. Have you got a list of things I need?"

Oooh, he was coming. It was time to get her crazy heart to stop beating so fast. "I'll make one before I leave tonight."

His brow pleated with confusion. "Tonight?"

"When we get back. Didn't I offer to help you move in if you came with me now? At this rate, it's going to be midnight if we don't hurry up," she said with an amusing smile. Then, with as much enthusiasm as she could muster, she asked, "Now, are you up for some exciting volunteer work?"

Instead of waiting for an answer, she turned towards the track, climbed over the fallen tree and continued on the home stretch. There was so much to be done at the tree roo park. How would they ever discover what was causing the tree roos to go blind? Without being aware of it, she lengthened her stride and quickly covered the last hundred metres.

Jack's footfalls were close behind. She struggled to keep her smile in check and her crazy heart at bay.

∾

Jack wasn't sure what he said, but he'd hit a raw nerve. For a split second, the energetic and determined woman disappeared. In its place, he glimpsed someone vulnerable and unsure. It unsettled him before he dismissed it as impossible.

She was rattling on about a research program, and he had to work hard to keep up with what she was saying. He dared another smile behind her back, finding it difficult to steer his gaze away from the tight curves of her backside. In thigh-length cut-off shorts, her shapely, muscled legs were also doing it for him, which was strange because she wasn't his usual type. Keeping his mind on what Eva was talking about was proving to be tough. The last thing he needed was his body to show any sign that she was turning him on.

He squinted when they passed through the forest's edge into a large clearing, not unlike his property. The afternoon sun bathed them in warmth as he surveyed Dr Karen's property.

A low-set brick home sat tucked to one side, and a farm shed leant precariously beside it. A small car and ute were in the garage, and under some trees on the opposite side near the property's driveway, another three vehicles were parked haphazardly. About two dozen caged enclosures, all two metres square, were sprawled around the yard and interspersed with the occasional tree providing some shade. Another little shelter on the side contained a couple of tables and an odd assortment of chairs. It resembled a workstation. Maybe where they prepared food for the roos.

A quick glance at some of the cages and it appeared they all contained a tree kangaroo, an old blanket, a water bowl and some greenery. He was becoming familiar with their golden-brown coloured fur, solemn black faces, ear, hands and feet, and their supposed glassy eyes that couldn't see too well.

"Hi, Karen," Eva called and waved to a woman, probably in her early sixties, and half-a-dozen young adults standing in a group, who replied with beaming smiles. "How is everyone?"

"We were just about to leave for the day," one young male volunteer said.

"Before you all disappear"—Eva tugged on Jack's arm so he was standing by her side—"this is Jack. He owns the adjoining property, so we have to be extra nice to him."

There were titters and chuckles from the group, but one young woman openly stared and ran an appraising eye over him. While this was something he was used to, he squirmed under her scrutiny while Eva stiffened beside him.

"That shouldn't be too hard," the young woman replied, making no effort to hide her interest. "How long have you been hiding this one, Eva?"

"Only met him yesterday, Laura." Eva's chuckle was strained.

What the heck? The last thing he needed was more unwanted female attention. If they thought his good looks came with a personality, they would learn soon enough. His dark moods usually scared them off; he'd been taking extra care not to frighten Eva.

"Hi, Jack." The older woman approached and offered her hand for a shake. Dressed in well-worn khakis, she reminded Jack of an older version of Eva. Tough, wiry and not scared of physical activity. Her short hair was a mix of brown and grey, and unlike Eva's smooth skin, her face showed the telltale lines of a woman beginning to age.

He took it and returned a firm shake.

"I'm Karen. Welcome to our tree roo rescue park."

"Thanks." He immediately warmed to her welcoming smile.

"Would you like a tour?" Dr Karen asked.

Jack nodded, leaving Eva's side to follow Karen to the first caged enclosure. Not before sending her a quick smile of thanks. For some reason, he wanted to reassure Eva he was her friend first. Didn't want her thinking that the good looks he inherited from his monstrous father could sway him so easily with the first pretty face to come along.

Why *this* was so important, he wasn't so sure because a pretty face had easily swayed him before.

CHAPTER 7

"We rescue about forty roos every year, but cars or dogs kill approximately fifty in the same period." A grim look shadowed Dr Karen's face.

Jack strolled around the property beside Dr Karen, strangely fascinated by her knowledge and enjoying the tour. She pointed out Kenny in one of the cages, reassuring him he was doing very well. "I heard you helped Eva rescue him."

He nodded. His days in Malanda were turning out to be so different from his usual days back home. When he wasn't flying, he was checking stock values, meeting with property managers, going over figures with the accountant, or looking into future investments. Being in the rescue park was far from his normal, but he enjoyed it.

Dr Karen squatted in front of a smaller cage, reaching in and removing a young roo. "This is Tommy. We found him tucked inside his mother's pouch after a car accident. When we get them at this age, they're not blind."

Eva appeared and gave Karen a small bottle filled with white liquid before disappearing again to complete other chores he assumed. "We don't let everyone handle the babies.

Eva and I mostly, and a couple of others are experienced enough."

While Karen settled back on an old rustic chair to feed the joey, Jack crouched down beside her and listened to the joey suckling. Unexpectedly, his chest tightened. He knew how hard losing a mother was. How often had he questioned his mother's reasons for leaving this world when *he'd* still needed nurturing? Even at the grand old age of thirty, it still hurt to be without her. He often ached for the comfort of her protective arms around him on his down days. She'd done the best she could, but nothing could protect them from the wrath of his father's rages when something set him off.

Jack shook his head. The urge to flee continued to live inside his head, so he rose and gave himself a mental shake. He settled in the seat beside Karen, needing to dislodge his thoughts. If left unchecked, they could trouble him for days.

Jack spotted Eva cleaning out an enclosure, and a sense of calm blanketed him as he watched her refill the water wells and rearrange the greenery. It eased the tension in his body, allowing him to unburden the thoughts that had momentarily plagued him. He forced his attention back to the doctor and asked a question that she *could* answer. "What's your current research telling you about their blindness?"

Karen used her free hand to stroke the joey between its ears. It was hard to overlook this woman's passion for these animals. It shone through her every action.

"The drought and climate change are stressing the trees in our rainforest and producing toxins in their leaves. Now when I say drought, I know it rains a lot up here, but the reality is that what was once a completely covered rainforested area is now just tiny clumps of rainforest. So, unlike an entire collective rainforest, the smaller clumps can't maintain the usual moisture a rainforest requires. Our research shows that the tree kangaroos are getting stressed from something, so we're leaning towards the toxins. This something is creating brain damage or optic nerve damage. But then again, we're not a hundred percent sure of this theory either. It could also be a virus."

"What happens to them once you've rescued them?" Jack reached over and scratched the joey behind the ear.

"Once we're satisfied they're okay, the blind adults go to zoos. We release these little ones back into the forest. But it'll take about two years before we do so."

Jack nodded, appreciating the years it would've taken to accumulate the bunch of tree roos roosting in the forest behind his house. Why were his possible plans to raze the house troubling him? The noise and disturbance would upset the serene environment Dr Karen and her band of volunteers worked so hard to create. Still, he couldn't dismiss his plans to build a rainforest retreat and sell it at the top market rate. It was one investment that hadn't paid him a single dividend yet.

"Here, Jack, have a nurse."

"Whoa." Shaken out of his reverie, he leant back, almost toppling the vintage cane chair. "I thought only the experienced volunteers did this job?"

"I did, but you come across as the sort who might enjoy it. Here …" Karen lifted the tiny joey wrapped in a soft rug and gently placed it on his lap. "Hold the bottle at this angle and let it drink at its own pace."

It happened too fast for Jack to argue. The small bottle looked like a toy in his large hand. Within seconds, the tiny tug of the joey sucking out the milk vibrated along his arm while he watched in awe. It was the strangest experience.

Tommy gave off a faint whiff of powdery fur, similar to a wet dog but not as strong. The scent hovered around Jack's nose, but he wasn't game enough to move or breathe in too deeply in case it startled the joey. He'd never held a baby, never experienced a younger sibling to teach him these things, never experienced the connection two humans, or a human and animal, could share. Not since his mother forced him to leave home.

As the tiny joey suckled, he realised how much he craved such closeness. The joey tucked inside the blanket was warming more than just the spot on his chest. He roughly swallowed and rapidly blinked a couple of times, not daring to tear his gaze away from the joey in case the sudden build-up of moisture showed.

The bottle was only half full, so he had time to get himself under control. He settled more comfortably in the chair, prepared to see it through to the end. He even lost the stiffness in his shoulders, unexpectedly enjoying the task.

"That's better, Jack. It takes a few minutes to get the hang of it."

Jack didn't look up at Dr Karen but nodded slowly to not startle the joey.

"I'd say he was a natural." Eva's unexpected closeness was enough for Jack to whip his head up. The joey jerked on his lap at the sudden movement before resettling. Jack didn't miss that look of sympathy again. Maybe compassion was what she did best; it would fit her rescue work. *Stop over analysing things. Why would she know anything about you?*

Karen left to put the kettle on for afternoon tea, and Eva settled into Karen's chair. "Adorable, isn't he?"

Jack managed a hint of a smile. He wasn't ready to let it bloom into a full one. Somehow this woman was worming her way into his life, threatening to change all his well-laid-out plans. "You think? I've seen cuter."

At that moment, Eva reached across to stroke the joey's

fur in the gentle manner Karen had used. When her hand touched his, a spark of electricity zapped along his skin, and his gaze flicked up to encompass hers. His breath hitched in his throat, Tommy on his lap forgotten for a moment. Who was he kidding? He'd held nothing as cute as this baby joey in his life. He'd also never met anyone as beautiful as this woman, which scared the hell out of him.

It was more than her looks—the thick, honey hair that was pulled back in a ponytail, the energy and the passion evident in her every word and action. The complete package was a very attractive deal, but he was yet to get his head around his plans. When he did, how would it affect everything Eva stood for?

He tore his gaze away from hers and concentrated on Tommy again. When the sound of Tommy's suckling changed to indicate the bottle was empty, Eva reached across and took the joey from his lap.

She rose and snuggled him against her chest. "How was that, Tommy? Ready for a nap?"

Eva smiled that blinding smile again and sent it in his direction. He greedily took every vestige of warmth it offered in case it never happened again. "I'll put him in his enclosure, and then we'll have a quick cup of tea before we leave."

He rose, stretched his arms above his head and gave her a slight nod. Dusk was approaching, and he had yet to decide where to sleep that night. Apart from the kitchen table setting and the old brown wardrobe, there was no other furniture in the house that he'd seen. But then again, he hadn't checked the rest of it. Either way, his custom-made swag on the front verandah sounded better by the minute.

Eva kept her pace brisk as they made their way back to Jack's house. She rarely left it this late in the day to make the trek, but there was enough light to make out the strips of flagging tape she'd used. Any later and they would've needed her torch.

"The roo park has received another government grant, which means we can send more brain samples away to be tested."

"You do that?"

"Yes, we do." They'd made it as far as her roo family, and it was impossible not to stop and check them. Lowering her voice, she added, "If a car hits a roo and survives, but the prognosis doesn't look good, we sacrifice it for research."

Jack shrugged in the shadows. She took another moment to scan the canopy. It was hard to identify them as they rustled from tree to tree, but being there was enough to buoy her spirits.

"Okay, time to go," she whispered, continuing along the track. "What did you have planned for dinner?"

"Dinner?"

"Ah, yup. Food, nourishment, that sort of thing."

A step behind her, Jack chuckled, deep, throaty. "I was going to the pub again. There aren't a lot of choices, are there?"

"How about you pop around to my place?" she asked when they stepped out of the forest. "I made a stack of chicken curry the other day, and it won't take much to cook up some rice to go with it."

Once they reached the cleared backyard, she spun around, walking backwards to catch what he said.

His step halted, and she did the same thing. "Thanks, Eva, but I shouldn't. I've wasted enough of your day."

"I could say the same thing," she said with a cheeky grin.

"It's only food." Why did she keep persisting? *Keep your mouth shut and forget about wanting another kiss.*

"Are you the town's welcoming committee?"

In the fading light, she couldn't tell if he was being sarcastic, funny or just plain annoyed. Well, she'd be all three if needed. "Does it matter? We all have to eat. Stop worrying about the mundane stuff. Have a plate of curry and go home. Simple."

"Oookay ..."

Jack dragging out the 'o' in okay caused her smile to slip. Was this going too far? She'd been foolish before with men, but this could be outright stupid if things went wrong.

"Simple is something you're not, Eva. But I love a good curry, so where do you live?"

She almost squealed with delight, like walking into sunshine for the first time. "Follow me, it's only a short drive away." *Keep it together, Eva.*

Even with Jack's history, there was this compulsion to throw herself at him. There was sorrow and guilt thrown into the mix too, but this was different. This was her every pulse coming alive whenever she was near him. There was the headiness that lifted her spirits into the clouds. She couldn't shut down because images of Jack swayed before her eyes. She wanted another kiss badly, but she didn't want to be thrown off Jack's property and unable to reach her roos. *Heck!* Now that she'd discovered how amazing a simple kiss from Jack was, what would be worse? Doing without her babies or never getting another kiss?

For the first time since discovering the connection she had with tree roos, there was something, or someone, who could threaten it and place her precious animals in second place. *Damn it! I can't go there.*

She inwardly groaned as she opened her ute door and

motioned for Jack to follow in his gleaming LandCruiser. She'd never encountered this problem before and had no idea how to deal with it. How precious were her babies? As Eva drove off, she drummed her fingers on the steering wheel, not having to think twice about her answer. Her tree roos were everything to her. So, this meant it was time to cool it with Jack until she got a better handle on his plans.

Okay, girl, strike off kissing for now.

CHAPTER 8

No sooner had Jack followed Eva into the cute cottage on the edge of town than she was at the fridge rummaging in the depths of the vegetable crisper.

The cosy but open living space boasted a single mahogany sofa in front of a television, a four-seat kitchen table and a small but workable kitchen. Cosy was something he'd long gotten rid of, replaced with chrome, glass and shiny. Eva's cosiness struck a chord like it was something he'd missed all these years.

He followed Eva into the kitchen, passing the short hallway that led to the other rooms. A hint of rosemary permeated the air. Jack turned one-eighty, taking in a couple of family photos hanging on one wall, a haphazard pile of glossy magazines spread across the sofa and a small coffee table beside it. He didn't have to read the title *What's Up* to guess what they were.

Then he spotted the giant teacup pot home to a rosemary plant. Nestled comfortably on the window ledge, it caught all the western sun in the afternoon.

"Here, Jack, wash these, cut this into strips and grate this."

Eva thrust a lettuce, capsicum and carrot at his chest.

"Use the sink. I'll get the rice started and dig up some naan bread from the freezer."

She disappeared towards the other end of the house. There one second, gone the next.

"The sink, Jack," she called back halfway down the hallway.

Her words prompted him to turn around and drop the vegetables into the sink. He could do this. He'd self-taught himself how to cook some basic meals. Not many. It wasn't a skill he needed. Not when his favourite restaurant cooked quality meals, often shared with work associates and the occasional woman. Salad wasn't high on his list, but he'd get the hang of it soon enough.

Rattling around in the top drawer, he found a knife. When Eva returned, she opened and closed a kitchen cupboard before placing a salad bowl on the side of the sink, followed by a grater and a vegetable peeler. With swift movements, she peeled the carrot and dropped it into the bowl. "There you go, ready to grate."

It took him the entire time it took Eva to set a pot to boil and cook the rice, to construct the salad. In the meantime, she placed the naan bread in the microwave to defrost and warm. Along with the curry reheating, the kitchen smelt amazing. His stomach rumbled loud enough to be heard over the whirring of the microwave.

"My bad, Jack. We should've left the roo park earlier. Sorry."

"With food that smells this great, what else did you expect my stomach to do?"

She chuckled. "Won't be long now, but please, don't let

me forget the washing. I just put it on." She rummaged in a cupboard, pulling out a colander to strain the cooked rice. "I hate leaving anything for the next day. I find I can't switch off if there's stuff still needing to do. What if something happened tomorrow and—"

"Eva, *please*!" Jack cut in, turning away from the sink to face her. She was back to the vulnerable woman he glimpsed earlier; she was like a deer caught in spotlights. He gulped, uncertain what to say now that he interrupted her. "Slow down," he suggested softly. "Let's face it, if something happened to you tomorrow, you wouldn't have to worry about the washing."

"Plates"—she pointed to a kitchen cupboard—"glasses, cutlery and serviettes over there."

Eva stirred the curry and drained the rice, totally ignoring his plea.

"And stop frowning. You can eat now."

"I wasn't frowning about that." Something about her vulnerability wasn't sitting well with him. But he attempted to loosen up and set the table. "I should've stopped at the pub for a bottle of wine."

Eva carried the rice first and then the curry and naan bread to the table. "Nah. Bitter crap and leaves a foul taste in your mouth. Not to mention it messes with the head when you've had one too many. She grimaced. Don't get me to recount my rebellious teenage days. By the next day, you'll regret what you said and did—if you remember any of it."

Jack's eyes popped open, and he burst out laughing. Eva froze behind the chair she was about to pull out. He reined in his laughter. "I haven't heard that take on drinking wine before." In his world, everyone drank wine with their meal.

"Hmm," she mumbled and sat, rearranging the hot food.

A quiet awkwardness settled between them as he joined

her at the table. *Come on, Eva, smile, laugh, talk nonstop.* What happened to the Eva of only that morning? Why had *his* sudden cheerfulness surprised her?

He didn't often laugh, but he *had* laughed at least once with her already. His stomach muscles still hurt from it. Or had he upset her by cutting in earlier? In future, he'd shut his mouth when she went vulnerable on him. Unless … unless she *was* dying. Some terminal illness he couldn't see.

"What?" she asked, trying to avoid his probing gaze.

"Just fighting off hunger pangs." He wasn't lying about that.

"Here, pass me your plate."

Jack did, and she began topping it up. A pain crossed his chest as he continued looking across at her. Why would he care? He had only met her the day before. But to imagine this beautiful, vibrant young woman, with more life in her than a dozen others put together, might be sick or physically hurt? He inwardly cursed. *Impossible!* She looked too healthy.

He halted the next spoonful when it looked like she wasn't going to stop. "Do I look like I need fattening up?"

She chuckled. "Sorry. I bet your stomach's hungry even if your eyes aren't"

That was better. Hopefully he'd dragged her away from the place that shook her up sometimes. He was the right man to know about this sort of thing.

He added a smile for her benefit. "I'm not about to argue with you." He *was* starving and didn't need any encouragement to tear up the warm naan bread and dunk it in the curry sauce.

He ate contentedly, amused by the size of Eva's helping. It wasn't far behind his. Surely someone sick didn't eat this heartily. Yeah, he'd gone completely off track. Something else bothered Eva, and anyway, it wasn't his business. For now, he enjoyed a rare homemade meal, eating every morsel. "This is delicious. Thanks. I would've made do with the same boring pub meal of steak and chips."

"Do you do much cooking?" she asked, setting her knife on the table. "Because there's a lady in town who holds classes. Worth your while, so you're not eating out all the time. Healthier too."

He poked at a piece of chicken with his fork. His plan to leave as soon as he could wasn't sitting as well as it should. At least she'd started to engage again. He'd managed that much. "Yeah, I cook some basic meals."

"Oops, give me a sec." She left the table and returned with a chilled jug of water from the fridge.

"I'm not as good a cook as you, I'm guessing?" Jack said, taking the jug from her and filling their glasses.

She smiled serenely when he looked up, and his heart somersaulted. It almost whooshed him back in his chair. The effect was so startling. You'd think he'd never dined out with a woman before. *Sheesh, get a grip, mate.*

"Some people procrastabake. It's a real thing," she continued, eating mouthfuls of curry in between her talking. "For me, it's therapeutic. When I can't sleep, or I'm thrashing out an article and it's not quite working, I bake cakes and biscuits or cook meals to freeze. This way, everything inside my head unlocks. When that doesn't work, I—"

"—visit your babies," Jack finished for her, his heart back in its place, even if it was beating a little faster.

She nodded, her thoughtful look doing his head in.

"If that doesn't work, do you have another option?" Jack asked, desperate to keep the conversation flowing and his mind off the way his traitorous body was reacting.

Eva tipped her head to the side, an unaccustomed frown digging into her brow. "Not really. I've never had to. My last resort always works, and in the meantime, my freezer is stocked with meals, and my friends benefit from my baking."

"I'll help you any day with the choc-chip biscuits." With a sudden pang, they reminded him again of how much they tasted like his mother's. He concentrated on his next mouthful, needing a few moments to get it together. At least it had the desired effect of dulling his desire. It was a good reminder it was time to deal with his ugly past. Would he get past it?

"Somehow, I eventually unwind the twisted mess of words I've created and make sense of it—*before* my deadline. Anyway, would you like some salad?"

Jack swiftly dragged his mind away from memories of his mother and viewed the mangled mix he'd chopped and grated. Suddenly, he was full.

"I have homemade dressing to go with it." Eva reached across the square table for the condiments sitting in a stylish carryall.

"Thanks," he said, changing his mind and reaching for the bowl. He supposed there were worse traits she could pester him about. Healthy eating was obviously one of hers.

Jack polished off the salad serving before putting his fork and knife down. "Thanks again. That was amazing." He scraped his chair back and rose. "If you show me where everything is, I'll do the washing up."

"No, leave it. I didn't help you unpack your car as promised, so you have enough to do before calling it a night."

Jack pushed his chair in, refusing to budge. "Well, it's either the washing up or hanging out the washing. Do you want me hanging up your things?"

A slight blush touched her neck as she slid her chair back and stood. "Okay," she agreed, looking away. "Everything is underneath the sink. It's not rocket science where things are kept."

Jack tilted his face and raked a hand through his hair. He managed a grin. "Yeah, but I'm male, and we don't always understand simple things like this." He was doing everything to get her to smile again just in case she shuttered herself away in that vulnerable place. He *had* spoken too harshly when he stopped her conversation earlier, and he wouldn't do it again.

"Am I missing something here?" A confused frown marred her beautiful face, and a sudden desire roared through his body. "Where do you keep *your* stuff for washing up?"

Jack gulped, hoping nothing showed. "Under the sink, of course. Where else?"

Eva rolled her eyes and made for the laundry. Three steps away, she stopped midstride and turned around. When uncertainty rippled across her face, an uneasy jab struck him. *What now?*

"Look, I'm not sure how to put this, but if you want to, you can stay for a hot drink, sleep in the spare room and sort out your sleeping arrangements tomorrow morning, but—"

His breathing hitched. Was this an invitation with a warning? When her gaze slowly locked onto his, it was impossible to look away or breathe. He made a rough sound to clear his throat before finishing for her in the most sensible way. "That would be crazy because we only met yesterday, and I wouldn't suggest such a thing." Too bad the desire to kiss her senseless just reared its head. Not a great idea. Not again. Not until he decided what to do with his home and property. Was his original plan already going to pieces?

That weird expression of sympathy crossed her face before her phone rang from the bench. She looked towards it, breaking the connection, giving him the chance to fill his lungs with much-needed air.

"Okay, you wash, I'll hang." She grabbed the phone and swiped it to connect the call, making her way to the laundry as she put it against her ear.

His shoulders dropped, and he let out a resigned sigh. *What is your problem, man?* Any of his mates would've taken up the offer and ended up in Eva's bed without thinking twice. But alarm bells rang loud, warning him not to go there. This whole predicament involving Eva, the property and the tree kangaroos was something to tread carefully around. To screw up after only two days?

He rocked back on his heels. He had no idea how it would end. Not until he stayed at the house. With that in mind, he wasted no time getting the sink clean. It was time to go home.

"No biking tomorrow, so you can sleep in."

Jack was drying his hands and spun around. So absorbed in his thoughts, he hadn't heard Eva return to the kitchen.

"It's been put off a day. Will you still want to come?" she asked, her expression hopeful.

Jack hung the tea towel on the oven door and nodded. "Sure." It was a pity. This meant he had all the next day to reacquaint himself with his childhood home. There would be no excuses, nothing to put off the inevitable. A shudder rattled along his spine. Sleeping in was what ordinary people did. Not those in a house where old ghosts would howl down at him. The nightmares might even return. There was only one way to find out. "Six am, still?" he checked, wiping his clammy hands on his jeans.

"Yeah, sure, I'll drop by your place and pick you up."

They stood staring at each other. It was awkward. How did you say goodbye? Kissing her seemed like the worst thing he could do, not with all the black memories jostling inside his head for a place at the front of the line. He might never come out the other side. "Thanks again, Eva. If you're game, I'll repay the favour one night."

"Are you going to be okay?"

Oh, hell. Why would she ask such a thing?

"There's just not much in that place of yours until your stuff arrives."

His fingers curled into fists, and he swallowed back a considerable lump. How had she guessed he could've done with the comfort of one friend that night? To be completely alone with whatever happened inside his head might leave him unhinged for a few days.

"Come here," she demanded. Before Jack could process anything, she wound her arms around his shoulders, giving him a tight hug. Enough to dislodge the broodiness that had threatened to engulf him only moments ago.

When she stepped back, she added, "You have my number if you need anything."

"Anything?" he blundered as a wave of emotion stole his ability to answer with something intelligent.

"Yeah, even milk for your coffee." She folded her arms and sent him a quick smile. Not her usual blinding stretched-across-the-face style, but a smile nonetheless.

"So, six am, then. The following day?" he confirmed one last time as he made his way to the front door.

"You got it! And thanks for all your help today," she called after him.

Right. He'd almost forgotten how full their day had been. Was it only this morning they hiked to Windin Falls? Was this a taste of what her life was like? Full on and nonstop?

Jack gave her one last wave. "I'll see myself out. You stay here." He closed the door behind him and made for his car. There was a flicker of sheet lightning in the sky. He didn't think anything of it, except for the small bead of sweat on his brow triggering the fact it might rain that night.

Resigned to whatever fate had in store for him, he ignored the humidity. Other things were occupying his thoughts, and with shaking hands, he opened the car door. He could do this. If it meant thinking of two kisses and one hug for the entire night, he would.

CHAPTER 9

Eva backed away from the front door and groaned. When her boot connected with the sofa, she slid her backside down beside it and covered her face. She rubbed her eyes and pinched her cheeks before impatiently tearing out the elastic band and letting her thick hair fall over her face. The tension release was immediate and soothing. Reaching up for one of the salmon-coloured cushions, she raised her knees and screamed into it for good measure.

What was it about Jack that had her acting in the most erratic way? If you took away his brooding good looks and the shock of jet-black hair against those startling blue eyes, what was it she'd never encountered with anyone else? Where the heck had the nonstop talking Eva gone? The one who didn't shut up and could keep the conversation light, funny and engaging for hours? *Yeah, right out the bloody window.*

Tightening her hands around the cushion, she fathomed what she saw in Jack's depths. For a second, she glimpsed a frightened little boy when she asked if he would be okay. Her heart had tripped over itself, going out to him in that hug. But it was only a flicker. He'd learnt how to hide behind his scowl, protecting himself with an impenetrable shield. Not even Laura's flirting at the roo park dented it. Did he know the effect he had on others?

Why the heck had he checked out of The Lodge so soon? There was only a kitchen table and an old wardrobe in the house, which was why she'd offered him her spare room. She groaned one last time before shoving the pillow aside and rising. As she wouldn't be getting any work done that night, she may as well bake a treat for the next day.

Needing to reschedule her day, she went searching for her phone. Jack would need a friend after spending the night alone, and she didn't want to turn up again until it was time to pick him up for the mountain biking. Acting desperate was the last thing she wanted to convey around him, but how long could she keep using her roos as an excuse?

She spun around on the spot, trying to recall where she had left her phone. *Come on, Eva, get it together*. Desperate she was, and it showed in the way her stomach flipped every time he managed one of his smiles. For God's sake, she'd only met him two days ago, but—yeah, the same shit over and over went through her head. She'd known of him for nearly five years—from the day she first drove into Harold's backyard, with all his regrets and helped *him* deal with his past.

She swore and made for the garage and the indoor laundry. Maybe the phone was there.

A gust of wind billowed the laundry curtain when she walked past. "What the—?" She pulled the window closed. That was the direction the wind blew when a storm was approaching. How had she not noticed any build-up earlier? It hadn't felt that humid. Or was her mind in other places?

She found her phone beside the laundry basket and rushed

back inside. She shut the windows as she went and kicked off her boots in the living room. When the first clap of thunder shook the house, she yelped, running the last steps to her bedroom and her usual hiding spot. Snatching the doona off her bed, she squeezed herself between the bed and the wardrobe and covered her head while pleading, "Not yet. Please not yet," over and over again.

"Bloody hell!" Jack didn't expect his first storm so soon. The thunder hadn't sounded that close when he cranked up the stereo in his LandCruiser for the short drive to the house—his way of drowning out the other noises in his head.

The storm halted his plans to sleep on the front verandah. He quickly dragged the swag inside the door and dropped it, his breathing laboured as though he'd just climbed a mountain with it over his shoulder. A crack of thunder rattled the house, and another flash of lightning lit up the room.

He hurried down the short hallway and flicked a cursory glance into all the rooms, only to confirm what he already suspected. They were bare. Taking a deep breath, he needed to confront this thing *now*. Only random light bulbs still worked, and the ones that did emitted a dull, yellow glow. The rain began its heavy drops, splattering on the roof, compounding the noises in his head.

In the living room, cooling gusts swept in from the windows he pushed open. Jack flapped the back of his shirt, giving him immediate respite. The fresh, moisture-filled breeze whirled around the room and mingled with the mustiness locked away for months. He took a moment to fill his lungs.

His greatest distress came from seeing the wardrobe

again. Not for the first time, he wondered what had gone through the warped mind of his father when he chose not to get rid of it. Or did he have dementia and someone else had cleaned out the house?

He shrugged, not caring what condition his father was in. The wardrobe would go the first opportunity he got. As his steps took him back to the bedrooms, there was nothing to hide the dents and repaired patches in a lot of places. As the lightning flickered around his periphery, each flash highlighted them all, one by one.

His chest shuddered at the crack in the wall near the toilet. The hammer had narrowly missed his mother that day. Another dent, a patch, a boot that time, a heavy Vegemite jar another time. Jack had smelt Vegemite for months despite how thoroughly his mother cleaned up the smashed glass and ugly black smear.

Every mark and scar became more pronounced without the furniture, and Jack hunched his shoulders as each memory seared his brain, bringing him back to those awful days.

He shuddered to think about his mother's state during her last days. He should've been there. Been man enough to stand up to his father and fight back. It was his biggest regret, and there would never be an opportunity to redeem himself.

On his way back to the living room, he stopped at a broken patch of Gyprock wall near the kitchen. Jack didn't remember the gaping hole. He remained glued to the spot, trying to recall the incident that had caused it. Nothing came. He'd memorised every other incident, so this must've happened after he left. With his hands clenched by his side, he tried his hardest to control the seething anger from erupting. If his father stood in front of him, he'd have strangled the bastard. How much had he hurt his mother that day?

On unsteady legs, he turned away and receded towards his swag, tasting blood from where he'd bit into his lip. A deep, unrecognisable growling sound escaped his mouth. He snapped. Like a broken marionette puppet, he collapsed with his legs askew. This was his fear all along. It was the proof he needed that keeping the promise to his mother was impossible.

The awful memories came flooding back as he curled into the foetal position on the wooden floorboards. Emotions tangled and thrashed. Fear, anger, loneliness. If only he hadn't been the frightened little boy. Like the big wave about to reach the shore, the emotions got too much, and years of pent-up frustration washed over him—and he bawled like he should have after learning of his mother's suicide a mere few weeks after she'd forced him to leave home.

The wrath and fury of the storm matched the one inside his head. As each minute passed, and the storm subsided, so did his. Slowly he rose from his crumpled form and shuffled back to lean against the wall. He ploughed both hands through his hair and left them there. He still had some sniffles, but the realisation that he had nowhere to go and no one to share it with saddened him. His family comprised only himself.

When the patter of the last few raindrops passed, Jack wiped his face on the bottom of his tee-shirt, rose on unsteady legs and went outside. He inhaled deeply the freshly invigorated forest and held it in before slowly releasing it. There *was* a family close by.

He opened the tailgate of his LandCruiser and found the raincoat and gumboots he purchased on his arrival in Malanda. Then he dug around further for the waterproof torch he always carried.

Shrugging the raincoat over his clothes and pulling the

gumboots on, he reached for a small tarp before slamming shut the tailgate. Then he trudged towards the backyard and into the dark forest where rain drops dripped off trees and landed on his face with a cool zing.

Jack sensed a patch of warmth on his right side. He'd wrapped the tarp securely around his body and had propped himself against a tree. He'd given the leeches free rein that night and wouldn't be surprised if there were entry marks where they'd fed off him before dropping off happily.

He'd easily found the family of tree kangaroos, had a quiet conversation with them, heard movement above and some light thudding as though some had left his morose company. Those were his last waking thoughts before exhaustion took over for a dreamless sleep.

Jack pried one eye open, and his jaw dropped. The warmth he sensed was the golden-brown fur of a tree kangaroo snuggled up against his side. A blast of the same powdery scent he smelt coming off Tommy rose to meet his nose. *Bloody hell!* He would have to move eventually, but he wouldn't yet.

Was this what it felt like to hold a child close? A loud squawk sounded overhead, and Jack flinched. The roo shot up, and within seconds it bounded into the undergrowth. Losing the warmth opened up a hollow cavity inside his chest. "Fuck."

Jack sighed and rose. He stretched the stiffness out of his back and folded the tarp. He had no idea what the time was, but he needed to charge his phone. With the power reconnected to the property, his next priority was connecting the internet and purchasing a fridge. A bed and selected pieces of furniture would arrive in a few days, making his life more comfortable until he decided what to do.

He tucked the tarp under his arm and checked his torch was still in the pocket of the raincoat, then looked up. "Thanks, guys," he muttered quietly. "How about we do this another time?" They peered down at him. What did he look like from that height? Was he a blurry mass? They were blind, weren't they? That's what Dr Karen and Eva kept saying.

He smiled unexpectedly. "My babies," he paraphrased Eva's words until the smile became his usual frown. How did he do anything to the property without disrupting the roos? He gave them a cursory wave and turned to the track. His footsteps sounded loud in the quiet morning as he trudged through the damp forest. He'd deal with it later. For now, he was starving, and the local bakery was next on his list of needs.

The morning sun glinted off a silver ute parked in the driveway. *Who now?* He wasn't in the mood for people. He was rumpled and needed a shower and a decent breakfast. If this was another roo-loving volunteer who wanted to spend a few minutes with their babies, he'd send them packing.

A man climbed out of the ute and strolled across the yard with a broad smile. Recognition came swiftly for Jack, and he shook his head in disbelief. The familiar coppery hair, the same crooked nose from a rugby scrum, the square jaw. "Mick Reynolds."

"Who the bloody hell else would it be?" Mick said, folding his arms.

"How did you hear I was back?" Were there no secrets in this town?

They exchanged a blokey hug before Mick stood back and tucked his hands under his armpits. "First, I hear the property's been sold. Total bullshit, I tell myself. Then in the same week, a video of Kenny the tree roo visiting the local hardware store goes viral and everyone's watching it. That's when I see a Jack look-alike in the video. So, I put two and two together, and here I am."

Jack smiled. The warmth of having his best mate close by touched a tender spot.

"And just so you know, you stink. You need a shower before I take you anywhere."

Jack poked his nose toward his armpit. Yep, he stunk. "Where are you taking me, and don't you have cows to milk?"

"Already done. I was up at the crack of dawn, as usual."

Mick's words couldn't hide the probing look he was giving Jack, and for a few moments, neither said anything. They took stock of each other. Jack tallied up the years and how they'd both changed from lean seventeen-year-olds into tall and well-built young men.

Dropping his arms, Mick asked, "You couldn't sleep inside?"

Jack nodded and removed his raincoat, letting it hang by his side.

"Ah … shit." Mick put his arm around his shoulder and squeezed. "Have a quick shower because I'm driving you home for breakfast. Jillian's cooking up a storm, and the two rug rats will keep your mind off things."

"A dad, hey?" A stab of jealously wrapped around his heart as they made for the house.

"It's the worst, trust me." His lips twisted into a wry smile. "Jillian's also heavily pregnant, so it'll be three soon."

"Yeah, I bet. So why do you look so goddamned happy about it?"

"Shit, is that how I look to you?"

Jack stopped at the verandah, turned to Mick and managed a grin. "Yeah, you do, and thanks; I needed a friend today, so thanks for looking me up."

Mick raked a hand through his tousled brown curls and grimaced. "I've missed having you around all these years. I wish you hadn't ditched me."

Jack dropped his head and swallowed. "I couldn't do it. I'm sorry, mate, I don't know why."

"Hey"—Mick reached across and squeezed his shoulder —"I get it. I know what happened. Your mum explained it to me before she …"

"Yeah … before she …"

Mick filled the awkward silence. "So, how about that shower?"

Jack managed another smile. It was easy to do around Mick. Like nothing had changed between them. "You know what, Mick? You're all grown up and a good-looking bastard to boot. Where'd you meet Jillian? Do I know her?"

"Nope. She's from down south. We met at an agricultural show in Brisbane."

"You were always a lucky bastard."

"Even luckier to have you back here. Like old times. What do you say?"

"I'm still deciding on it."

"Well, I'm rooting for you to fix this old place up and follow in the footsteps of your best mate. Go one better in the number of kids."

"Bloody hell, I'm going to run." And they laughed in their old, relaxed way.

"Don't you dare!" Mick gave him another friendly slap on the shoulder and pointed to the house. "Go now. I'll have Jillian on my case if we don't hurry."

Grinning, Jack climbed the steps with more vigour than he'd woken up with, buoyed by having his old mate beside him.

"By the way, dress up a bit swanky. We run a farm stay on the dairy property, and a photographer is coming to take some shots. We'll get one of you feeding the calves or something."

Jack shook his head and walked inside. At school, Mick had been the ideas man. It seemed nothing had changed, which gave Jack another reason to smile and get a move on.

CHAPTER 10

"Okay, Johnny, hold the bucket nice and tight while the calf feeds." Eva directed Mick's oldest son for the photos she wanted, totally absorbed in the joy of creating a new image. It captivated all her attention, taking away from any thoughts troubling her. It helped to erase the scare of the storm the previous night.

The cuteness of Johnny grabbed at her heart too. Dressed in jeans and gumboots, with the standard red and black checked shirt, it was hard not to hug this adorable human. His cheeky smile, topped by a head of chocolate-coloured curls, added to it.

"Eva, is this right?" Johnny asked in his five-year-old voice.

She gave him the thumbs up from behind the camera, and his dimpled smile stretched further.

"So, you're the town's photographer, too?"

Eva jumped at Jack's voice behind her, and she missed the shot.

"Breakfast, everyone!" Jillian called from the farmhouse.

Johnny dropped his pose, leaving the bucket behind, and ran to his mother.

Every nerve ending sizzled. She spun around so fast, stumbling on a clump of dirt.

"Whoa, careful there." Jack's voice tickled her neck as his arm scooped around her waist, stopping an inevitable fall.

A warmth crept up Eva's throat. She needed to get herself together. Fast. Ignoring the speed her heart was beating, she pulled out of Jack's vice-like grip, removed the camera strap from around her neck and plastered the biggest and breeziest smile across her face. "Good morning, Jack. I didn't expect to see you here today?"

"Yeah, same here," he said, shoving his hands into his jean pockets.

Eva busied herself by flicking through the photos she'd taken. "I do some freelancing on the side. It keeps me in the game."

"Mick's an old mate. He spotted me on Kenny's rescue clip. Apparently, it's gone viral."

Why did Jack feel the need to explain his presence? She dangled the camera on her wrist and looked up. "Mates, hey?"

"Yeah, years ago. Haven't seen each other since. Found where I was hanging out and turned up."

Eva nodded and picked up her tripod and camera bag. She'd asked Mick to check up on him after a night alone in the house. Jack deserved the truth. Guilt gnawed at her, but she let it slide for now. She learnt of this old friendship by chance. Eva had mentioned something about Harold's son returning and her concerns about the tree kangaroos. A detailed discussion had followed, leaving Eva in no doubt that she had an ally in Mick. Someone else who would do anything to help Jack. "Looks like breakfast is ready. Jillian's a fabulous cook, and it's the highlight of coming here." Eva just hadn't expected Mick to invite Jack along for the photo shoot.

Jillian's menu encompassed the standard continental breakfast Jack would find at any five-star hotel. Bacon and eggs, mini sausages and tomatoes, toast and jams, fruit juice and cereal if he could fit it in. The food was delicious and, like Eva's curry the night before, it hit the spot perfectly. Jillian brewed a good, strong coffee for him, and Mick filled him in on the current ups and downs of the dairy industry.

"You'd be surprised how busy the farm stay side of things is. We fixed up an old cabin on the creek, and every man and his dog from the coast is queueing to come. I'm thinking of rigging up a second one. Are you hanging around long enough to give me a hand?"

Jack chuckled at Mick's enthusiasm. It wouldn't be million-dollar stuff, but it was hard to discount the quality of life it brought Mick and his family. It was enough to make any man envious. "Just name the date." There'd been many times when Jack had hung out with Mick to escape his father's wrath. It was time to pay it forward.

"Eva, I thought we could use Jack in some shots," Mick said. "Jillian's not too keen with her extra-large belly."

Eva giggled at the good-natured scowl Jillian sent to her husband. Jack sat transfixed while Eva balanced Johnny on one knee and the toddler Trevor on her other. They clambered up and down like they'd done this a thousand times before. Something in Jack's chest twisted as he watched Eva at ease with the kids.

"What will we have him doing, Mick?" She directed a

cheeky grin in Jack's direction, and his stomach did its usual flip.

"Anything that won't dirty his clothes. Those jeans look like they cost more than my latest tractor. I won't be able to afford to replace them." Mick whistled between smiling lips.

"Maybe you should loan me a pair of yours?" Jack joked back. His jeans had cost him a pretty penny, but they were comfortable and a long way from the few items of clothing he owned when he'd left here. Repeatedly repaired and let out, patched and washed until the dye no longer came out. As with everything, his mother had done the best she could.

Jillian rose and rubbed her side. Mick rose too. The look of adoration Mick gave her spoke a thousand words. "Will you be okay if we leave you to clean up here, love?" Mick asked.

"Take those two monsters with you and everything will be fine," she said, smiling at her two young sons.

"Johnny, Trevor, can you both go to the bathroom and wash your hands. We need to finish the photos," Mick said to the boys.

The two boys protested but reluctantly climbed off Eva's lap and trundled down the passage.

Mick looked back and said, "I'll give Jill a quick hand and sort out these boys. If you want to start with Jack's shots, Eva, I'll try to tidy them up again."

Jack's shoulders dropped. How the heck was this going to work? "Am I supposed to smile in these things?"

Eva chuckled as she collected her gear. "Follow me, Jack. I'll tell you when to smile."

"Follow her directions, Jack. Our Eva can get feisty if you don't do as you're told."

Jack grumbled as he rose and pushed his chair in. He was the last person wanting to model in a photo shoot and had been caught off guard by Mick's appearance that morning. Maybe this was all a con job and Mick had used the temptation of food to get him on side. No different from how Mick had used his mother's great cooking back in the day to convince Jack to help out.

"Thanks for breakfast, Jillian," Jack remembered to say to her retreating back.

She turned and smiled, resting her hand on her protruding stomach. "Any time, Jack. Cooking's a pleasure. Eva's cooked us a treat for morning tea, though. I hope you can stay that long?"

It was as though the past thirteen years had never happened. Mick turned his way and gave him a wink. *Bloody hell!* How often had he used the same manoeuvre in the past? 'Jack, do you want to give me a hand with the fencing?' 'Jack, we could do with a spare pair of hands, we're spraying the cattle today.' 'Jack this … Jack that …' Mick was always up to something and providing a decent meal had always been his way of thanking him. He smiled and made for the kitchen door leading outside, where Eva had already gone. Some bastards never changed.

When he caught up with Eva, he asked, "When did you cook the treats for morning tea?"

She froze before resuming her equipment preparation. "After the storm."

It was none of his business, but the words had a mind of their own. "Couldn't you sleep?"

Setting up the tripod took all her attention, and she didn't look his way. "The storm unnerved me a bit."

"It caught me by surprise too."

"Did you sleep well?"

"I spent the night with your babies."

Her breath whooshed out of her mouth while her face

whipped up. "With my babies?" They stood only millimetres apart, and her familiar light scent assailed his senses, reminding him of biting into a freshly picked strawberry.

Jack nodded. "I woke up to find one snuggled beside me."

Her mouth opened with an 'oh'. "No way, you're lying."

He forced his gaze to move away from that mouth and travel to her eyes. Once they latched onto them, his breath forced its way out slowly.

"You couldn't sleep in the house?" she asked softly, that look of sympathy flickering across her face again.

He swallowed roughly. "I just needed some space. I found it with your family." *Shut up. Don't say anymore.*

His face dropped a fraction while every warning siren rang out loud. *Don't do this.* He told himself to shut the fuck up and touched her sweet lips with his. Eva tensed for a nanosecond before relaxing. So, he took it a little further, his tongue darting inside her mouth, while he tightened his hold on her arms. He filled his empty core with everything Eva, just in case he screwed things up and never got the opportunity again.

They jumped apart at the sounds of Johnny and Trevor's excited laughs from the house and Mick's stern voice asking them to stand still while he combed their hair.

Jack groaned, his eyes never leaving her face. Eva took in a gulp of air and straightened her shoulders. "Right, I want you to gaze over the fence towards the paddock. Look serene as though you're enjoying the amazing scenery. No smiling required in this one."

"What if the amazing scenery is behind the camera?" he asked with raised eyebrows.

"Don't, Jack. I have a job to do." She took a step back.

"So do I, and it's not this."

"You'll be perfect for the shots. You'll have tourists

screaming to get here if they think they'll find someone like you."

Jack grumbled, missing the touch of her lips like a person missed a good night's sleep. "They'll have to rely on Mick's good looks."

"He's already taken."

"Shame. I'm not good at this sort of thing."

"I'll make you good. Now shut up and start doing as you're told."

"Bossy," he uttered, not in the least bit affected by it. He positioned himself with his side facing the camera and smiled at her bluntness. Mick hadn't been joking about her feistiness. The shutter clicked continuously in the quiet morning air, so maybe he had the pose right even if he was smiling. Who would know? This wasn't something he'd done before.

He risked a glance, turning to get a glimpse of what she looked like behind the camera, and she swore.

"Do! Not! Move! Not until I say so. Keep your face turned towards the open spaces. Remember, there's only you, the cows and the mountains."

His unexpected laughter bellowed out into the air. This time, the camera clicking sounded ballistic. Luckily, the boys and Mick turned up, and the busy morning continued with no more awkwardness between them.

Her collection of photos included the animals, dairy, sheds and equipment, all captured with the incredible scenery of green rolling hills, patches of rainforest and the serene blue mountain range in the distance. By the end, Jack joined Mick in carrying one boy each on their shoulders, like Jack had done it a thousand times before.

Except he'd done no such thing. With a suddenness that struck him hard at his core, he realised all the money in the world couldn't buy him this.

CHAPTER 11

Eva gave herself an extra twenty minutes. Enough time to check on her babies before leaving for the mountain biking. She glanced out the ute window as she approached Jack's house. The sun looked a little shaky that morning with a hint of drizzle threatening. The bike track was a good half-hour drive away towards the drier end of the Tablelands, which boded well. Wet and slippery conditions were not ideal when wheeling down rough tracks.

At the house, her headlights caught Jack in their beam, and her breath came out in a gasp. She jerked straighter behind the wheel and crawled the last few metres. On the front verandah, he sat up in his swag; his eyes opened wide in alarm.

She hastily turned off the ignition and got out of the ute.

Jack scrambled around for his phone and glanced at the bright light. "Christ, Eva, I'm sorry. I got everything ready last night but forgot to set the alarm." He got to his feet and ploughed a hand through his sleep-mussed hair. "I've got a few minutes, haven't I?"

Her heart dropped. Did Jack get any sleep? His bloodshot

eyes and tired lines suggested a rough night. "You have. I'm going to check on the roos. I'll be back in fifteen minutes."

Jack dragged his swag inside. "I'll be ready, I promise."

Eva smiled wistfully, and it was enough to do the trick. His shoulders relaxed, and he looked less agitated. A smile even tugged at the corner of his lips. "It's hells job keeping up with the nonstop Eva Stamford. I should've stayed awake all night just to make sure I was ready."

"How do you know my surname?" she bantered back.

"Ah … best mate and all. After you left the farm yesterday, we talked of nothing else."

She cocked her face and arched a brow. "Yeah, right."

"Well, we might've touched on some other topics, as blokes do. Now get going; you're eating into my prep time here."

Eva laughed and turned towards the backyard, swallowing back the emotions trapped in her throat. Mick didn't know her full story, so she was safe there, but what sort of night had Jack experienced? He hid a lot behind light-hearted talk and his usual frown, but she read so much in his expression with her surprised early arrival. She'd seen pain, anguish and futility.

It didn't bode well if Jack couldn't handle the bad memories of his past. He still couldn't sleep inside the damn house, which concerned her. What if he sold the property to a savvy developer who saw its resale potential? There might be no saving the tree roo reserve they worked so hard to establish. Somehow, she had to help Jack.

She retrieved the small torch from her front pocket and switched it on. The morning sun only managed a few streaks past the tightly knit canopy. Already midway through spring, the days were lengthening, and she didn't need to add tripping over an exposed tree root to her morning. She wanted to enjoy the adrenalin rush that trail bike riding gave her. It was all part of her motto to live every day because it could be her last.

"Shit." She was halfway to her family of roos before realising she'd left behind her safety glasses and long gloves in the ute. On the off chance some of her babies remembered her and came closer, she would have to stand back. She'd also rushed off without one of three trusty yoga mats she kept in her vehicle. Eva rubbed the back of her neck, resigned to finding the driest spot to sit and unwind.

When she arrived, she changed her mind and crouched instead, leaning against a moss-covered trunk and filling her lungs with the strong, earthy smell. Slowly exhaling and relaxing, she turned her gaze away from the hundreds of tiny green ants that scurried up and down the length of the rainforest native.

She looked up and whispered, "Good morning," and watched in usual awe at how her babies went about their lives as the new day emerged—moving from tree to tree, eating leaves, protecting their young. Her family, Jack had said, and it was true. They were the closest she had when her real one was far away in Brisbane.

She closed her eyes for a few minutes, taking in more of the pungent smell surrounding her. It always invigorated her mind, but that morning she struggled for absolute calm. The look on Jack's face on her arrival took centre stage behind her closed eyelids. It was hard to unsee the pain she'd witnessed. She took slow, steady breaths and tried to will it away, but it wouldn't budge.

"Hey, there."

Her eyes whipped open, and his arrival startled her enough to drop to her backside. "Jack," she gasped in the early quiet, pressing her hand to her thundering heart.

"Did you forget this?" Jack unrolled one of her yoga mats. "And sorry, I didn't mean to frighten you, but I spotted them in your ute the other day and noticed you didn't have one with you."

She sat transfixed on Jack's face and couldn't move. He'd gone from rumpled to fresh-faced so fast it couldn't be the same person.

"Come on, shove over so I can get this thing underneath us both."

His closeness left her entirely devoid of defences. Jack half lifted her, plonked her back on the mat, and seated himself close enough that their shoulders barely touched. A wispy sense of pine and a freshly showered smell wavered in the air around him and warmed a sensitive spot. She inhaled a little more, letting it overtake the stronger forest smell. Then she did the silliest thing and leant right in and rested her head on his shoulder.

Then, even crazier, she uttered the same words she had the other night. "Jack, are you okay?"

He tensed, and the seconds before he answered lasted an eternity. "Not really," he mumbled.

"Do you want to talk about it?" After more silence, her face dropped into her hands. "Sorry, it's none of my business."

"Are you the town's psychologist, too?" He asked, seriously.

Her face flicked up, and she swivelled to face him better, falling into the dark pools of his eyes. Some resolve strengthened in her, and she drew her shoulders back. "Maybe I am." She needed to hear his story from his lips. She knew Harold's version.

"I used to live in that house. The memories are not good,

and I'd rather not say any more here. I don't want to spoil this spot."

His gaze remained riveted to hers, causing her chest to heave with all the emotions flickering across his face. With a softened resolve, she whispered, "I've been told I'm a good listener."

Jack eased himself back against the tree trunk and closed his eyes. Eva held her breath. Had she crossed the line? Was she being too intrusive? She'd never forgive herself if Jack told her to go away and never come back.

Jack's mouth twitched, and the possibility of a smile hovered around his mouth. "Are you sure?"

Eva's groan reverberated around them. It was enough to break the tension and draw the conversation away from Jack's past. Her ability to talk wasn't anything new.

She'd entirely forgotten about her babies and heard movement and rustling again. The roos were better visible now as the rising sun filtered more of its rays through the canopy.

Jack chuckled. "I know, you're being too loud. Maybe if you didn't talk so much—"

Eva whipped her face back to Jack and feasted on one of his rare smiles. It was enough for her laughter to bubble forth. They'd done this once before but surely not now after Jack's admission.

"Oh, no you don't. Not again, Eva; you're supposed to stay quiet here," Jack hissed as he struggled to keep a straight face.

There was no stopping her, though, and Jack took this as his cue to draw her into his arms and muffle her laughter.

Her laughter had barely settled when she sprung up on unsteady legs. "Jack, we have to get going, or we'll be late."

Jack was up in a flash, rolled the yoga mat and tucked it under his arm.

"Can … can we talk later?" she stuttered, unsure how to tackle Jack's declaration.

Jack took her hand and squeezed it once. "Okay."

Jack chuckled underneath his helmet. These people were crazy. This was the easy trail? Bloody hell. What did the experienced rider's trail look like? Jack didn't want to find out. Once again, Eva showed him up in both skill and stamina. He had a lot of catching up to do if he wanted to keep up with the unstoppable Eva Stamford.

In fact, he'd never felt so inadequate around a woman before. For reasons he couldn't explain, despite Eva being incredibly different from what he thought he wanted in a woman, there was a magnetic pull that kept drawing him towards her.

Jack stood with feet firmly on the uneven ground, rolling the borrowed bike back and forth while waiting for the group to finish talking. It was enough to stir the dust on the track. As the breeze eddied and swirled around his feet, he picked up a hint of burnt ash. Trees close by had suffered through a bushfire or back-burn.

They'd ridden twenty-five kilometres, and he eyed the final descent to the end of the trail. Eva looked back to check he was ready to go. He gave a thumb up and took a big breath. A broken bone was the last thing he needed. He'd be taking it nice and steady.

"Okay, everyone, let's finish this. Breakfast awaits us," Darryl, the organiser, called out.

Jack used his gloved hand to mop the sweat build-up on

his brow. Too late, he realised mud streaked his gloves, which would now be pasted across his forehead. He grimaced. He'd be a fine sight at the bottom if he made it in one piece.

They all took off in an excited rush. Jack followed at his own pace, already thinking twice about ever attempting this sport again. The rushed laughter and shrill calls from the others as they sped down the remaining track whipped past him. It was only a short stretch, but he gasped and braked hard when one of the bikes in the lead pack rolled over itself and spun down the remaining metres. The rider followed in the same somersault fashion.

"Eva!" someone shouted, and his breath caught.

"Christ!" Jack sped towards the end of the track, not caring about his safety. When he reached the group, Eva was sitting up and rubbing her shoulder.

He knelt as close as possible to Darryl. "Eva, are you alright?"

Her smile was a little crooked as she rubbed her arm. "I think a sharp rock stabbed my arm."

A blob of blood had already seeped through her bike shirt.

"But the rest of me feels fine."

"Give yourself a few minutes to make sure you're not concussed," Darryl insisted before directing the riders to take the bikes to the car park about a hundred metres away. Then he moved Eva's limbs and told her to close her eyes and open them again to check for concussion.

"I'm fine, Darryl, honestly," Eva maintained.

"I'm sure you are, but I'm checking you over anyway," Darryl asserted. "Do you think you can stand up?"

"I'll carry her back to the ute and drive us home," Jack said gruffly.

"Jack, no, not necessary," Eva pleaded.

"Too bad, Eva Stamford. I get to be boss until we make

sure you're okay." Now that he knew her surname, he liked the ring it had when he used it.

"Wouldn't hurt, Eva," Darryl said.

Eva groaned her frustration and rose on unsteady legs. She looked shaken, and Jack swooped in to lift her. "Put your arms around my neck, please. I have no intention of dropping you."

His knees turned to jelly when she swept her gaze in his direction. She was tense and careful not to rest her face against his. Pity, because he would've liked that. He carried her petite frame as he gently jostled her more comfortably in his arms. "Is that okay?"

When she smiled shyly, his knees threatened to buckle. He swallowed when she nodded and forced his stilted legs to move towards the car park. Within metres, her head fell towards his shoulder, and he almost let out a sigh. Strangely, she had nothing to say, and he desperately wanted her to talk about anything. If they'd been alone, there'd be no guarantee he wouldn't turn his face and kiss her. Or nestle his face in the crook of her neck and inhale the dust and sweat of their morning's exertions. It was starting to turn him on, but he needed to switch those thoughts off. His breathing sounded loud, and Eva would either think he was struggling to carry her, which he wasn't, or something else. With the chemistry buzzing between them, he could've sworn her breathing didn't sound normal either, but he wasn't game enough to look her way.

One step at a time. He'd already admitted to not being okay. How would she react when she knew his story? He couldn't explain how the nightmares the previous night had left him rattled. A shudder rippled over his body at their reminder, and Eva lifted her face to look at him.

Luckily, they arrived back at the car park, and Jack placed

her steadily back on her feet. The questioning look Eva gave him had him biting his bottom lip. He turned away and went to help tie the bikes down while Darryl did another check over Eva.

He'd agreed to open up. Apart from the snippets Mick knew of his past, he'd never fully opened up to anyone before, including therapists.

Would he finally be able to do it?

CHAPTER 12

Eva needed Panadol and a good sleep. The fall hurt more than her pride, and a few places over her body were tender, but thankfully no broken bones. When she untangled her limbs at the bottom of the descent, her heart had boomed for more than one reason. She didn't need reminding that her thirtieth birthday was fast approaching.

Eva was happy with the number of photos she'd taken along the way. Luckily, Darryl had offered to carry her compact camera on the ride, so there was no damage and nothing to hold up her next edition. They all enjoyed a barbecued breakfast before returning the borrowed bikes, and now Jack was driving her ute back to his place. It was an over-the-top reaction because she was more than okay to drive. But Darryl had sided with Jack, and she couldn't be bothered arguing.

She must be feeling off!

"My new fridge is being delivered today," Jack said, breaking into her musings.

This perked her up. It meant some sort of permanency, didn't it? Of course, she had no idea how long he planned on staying in the area. He had a job, and she assumed another home to return to. You couldn't be a pilot from Malanda. Cowpats didn't make for suitable runways.

"What about mundane stuff like plates, forks and knives? Is anything arriving with your gear?" Eva asked, twisting under the constraints of the seatbelt to face Jack.

They approached his rainforest-lined drive, and Jack indicated to turn in. As the dappled shadows fell over the ute, his shoulders sagged.

"Not really. I wasn't sure what I'd need."

"Would you like a hand? I could come with you," Eva offered.

Even without any sun shining in through the windows, it was hard to miss the thankful smile he flicked her way as he negotiated the driveway.

"Or at least suggest where the closest place is to buy such things," Jack said.

Eva nodded. "Starting with nothing requires some thought. I could make a list of the basics." She assumed Jack had expected to find the house fully furnished. He wasn't to know the complete turnaround Harold had gone through the past few years and Harold's reasons for giving Jack a blank canvas.

"I've started with nothing before; I should be able to do it again." Jack's hold tightened over the wheel, and her heart bled for the young man who had faced the world alone.

"Shit!"

Huh?

Jack slammed on the brakes. She twisted back to face the front. An unfamiliar vehicle was parked in the yard, and three people stood around it. Eva didn't recognise them as locals.

"Are you expecting visitors?"

"Maybe. But not this soon." His words were barely audible.

Jack emerged slowly from the ute, and Eva waited a few moments before doing so. As Jack closed the door, he gave her an apologetic look through the open window, which didn't make sense. Then it became startlingly clear.

A delighted squeal pierced her ears when Eva hopped out. One of the two females flung herself at Jack and wrapped her arms around his neck.

"It's so good to see you again, Jack."

"Stef, guys, I wasn't expecting to—"

Before Jack could finish his sentence, Stef planted her mouth on his with a passionate kiss to rival the best. Eva couldn't pull her eyes away, her mouth agape, while the other two people chuckled in the background.

It didn't look like Jack minded either, but he eventually drew Stef's arms away and stepped back. "Er … guys, great to see you all. I wasn't expecting you this way so soon."

The guy spoke first. "When they pushed me to attend a conference in Cairns, I invited these two to come with me. With a free day to visit tourist spots, we decided to venture into the wilds and find you."

"And what an adventure it was, Jack, finding this place. A bit colonial, isn't it?" the second woman said. She had her arm wrapped around the other guy's shoulder, and Eva took them as a couple.

Jack must've remembered Eva's presence. He fidgeted with the keys before rubbing the back of his neck and turning to beckon Eva closer. "Everyone, this is Eva."

Eva didn't move at first but then took tentative steps towards the visitors.

"Eva, this is Brad, Brittany and Stef." Jack pointed to each one in turn.

"Who is she, Jack?" Stef half-joked, but her probing glance studied Eva.

Jack shuffled his feet and nudged a rock on the ground with his shoe before chuckling and looking up. "Eva's many things. She's been showing me the area and taking me on adventures. I'm pretty sure she's not scared of anything."

"I'm scared of one thing," Eva mumbled under her breath when Jack wouldn't look at her.

"And she's passionate about saving the tree kangaroo," Jack added, turning his gaze in her direction for a fleeting moment.

"A what? A kangaroo that lives in a tree? Never heard of it," Brittany added to the conversation.

What a surprise! She took a step back. Stef was scrutinising her and wouldn't have missed her dirt-streaked face. Nor would the bloodstains on her sleeve be easy to overlook. Compared to the newcomers' designer pants, labelled shirts and expensive leather shoes, she'd never felt so out of place. The hire car was also a luxury model designed for those with money to throw around.

Eva braced her stomach and straightened her back, pasting a gigantic smile across her face. She could do this. "It's lovely to meet you all." Turning to Jack, she added, "I'm expected at the rescue park later today, and I have my edition to finish. I better get going."

She turned away before he felt obliged to say anything. At the ute, she opened the door and hopped in, only to discover the keys weren't in the ignition. She was about to let out a groan when Jack's face appeared in the open window. He dangled the keys in front of her face.

"Don't go, Eva. It's not what you think."

She snatched the keys. He hesitated for a fraction of a second before letting her take them. "I think I should."

She inserted the key and started the engine. Its sound was deafening in the quiet yard but not as loud as the noises in her head. By the time she manoeuvred a three-point turn to drive away, Stef had already reclaimed Jack. She'd wrapped her arms around his waist, and their bodies were pressed together. It looked like Stef was reluctant to ever let him go. Eva gave a cursory wave in their general direction and forced herself not to look in the rear-view mirror as she drove away.

She bit into her bottom lip and fought the fresh wave of tears that stupidly threatened. What was she thinking? So what if her feelings for Jack were getting out of control. She would handle the gut punch of seeing Jack kiss someone else, even if it killed her. But how could *he*? He'd kissed her, hadn't he? Was Stef his girlfriend or was he this friendly with all women? With her birthday only weeks away, it was better she found out sooner. This morning's tumble down the hill was warning enough.

Jack gritted his teeth and turned to face his friends. He wanted to shout at them, but that wasn't his way.

Extracting Stef's arm from around his waist, he held her at arm's length and raised his eyebrows. Her expensive perfume caught in his throat, and he coughed to clear it. "Stef, that was totally unnecessary."

"Oh, Jack, one day you might see me differently. I was doing you a favour. She's a bit provincial, isn't she? And the mud covering her body. Did it rub onto you?"

"Remind us how many days you've been here, Jack?" Brad asked. "And already you're collecting a trail of women a mile long."

Jack shook his head, worried about the impression they'd

given Eva. He rubbed a hand over his mouth, still stunned by the display Stef made by kissing him. It wasn't the first time she'd more than hinted about taking things further.

"We had a look inside, Jack. Not a lot to hold onto if you ask us," Brittany said as she walked up to the verandah and ran her hands along the old balustrade. The other two followed Brittany back inside the house, leaving Jack alone with his thoughts as he slowly followed.

Three days. *Three bloody days,* and for the first time, his closest friends were rubbing him up the wrong way. What was wrong with Brit? Hadn't she noticed the intricately carved tulips in the balustrading? He traced a tulip petal with his finger. His grandfather carved those by hand. *By bloody hand!* Didn't this silver-spooned bunch of snobs see that?

The real question was, had he been this much of a snob three days ago?

Jack sighed, seeing it all through Eva's eyes for the first time. He was one of them. Hadn't he had a private whinge to himself about getting covered in dirt that morning, despite the adrenalin rush he'd experienced? Not to mention the great physical workout, the spectacular views from the top of the hill, and the friendship with honest everyday people who did things differently from his usual crowd.

He followed the trio inside. They were opening doors and peering around. With bated breath, Jack waited for their questions about why the walls were so marked and patched. But nothing came. His open, messy suitcase and some boxes were still piled up in the living room where he'd left them. His swag was a tangled mess from when he dragged it inside earlier.

Not embarrassed by the mess, the rumpled swag reminded him of holding Eva in his arms and muffling her laughs. He smiled and enjoyed the rush that tingled over his skin. He hoped his friends didn't notice anything as they took in his squalid living arrangements.

"Knock it down," Brad suggested. "Build the perfect rainforest hideaway with all the mod cons and then sell it and make a killing."

Jack looked away and chewed on his bottom lip when an unusual emotion speared his chest.

"Hey, mate, you're not seriously thinking about keeping it, are you?" Brad asked, coming to stand in front of him. Jack tried to maintain a neutral look, hoping not to give anything away.

"Didn't your grandfather build it or something?" Stef asked.

Jack sagged against a doorframe to one of the bedrooms and looked anew at his friends. "Yeah, he did, so I want to think about it carefully." What did they understand about the house? It didn't do glossy, chrome surfaces and modern paint schemes, so it didn't interest them. It wasn't the sort of place to fill with plush leather couches and knick-knacks sourced from specialty antique shops. As for expensive artwork dotted around its walls, nah, it wouldn't work. Now for the importance of the tree roos—yeah, they wouldn't understand that either.

But only a short time ago, his line of thinking aligned with those of his friends. He'd worked so goddamned hard all these years, so he could afford what he wanted. Would he be happy with a place like this if he kept it? He couldn't blame their pessimistic warnings. He aspired to the same dreams, covering up an impoverished childhood he wanted to forget.

"So, where are you guys staying?" Jack pushed himself away from the doorframe and led them back outside. There was nothing to offer them in the house, and a bit of panic had stifled him. Maybe Brad was right. If he couldn't stand to be inside, perhaps it was better off to sell.

"At a nice resort on the Esplanade," Stef said.

"Which means we have to drive down that winding road again to get back there. Ugh! It gave me horrible car sickness on the way up," Brittany added.

Back out on the verandah, Jack held in a chuckle. The road leading from the coast to the Tablelands was like that.

"So, we thought we'd find a nice restaurant, have lunch with you and then make tracks back," Brad finished for them.

"It'll have to be the pub," Jack offered. He wasn't hungry and rather hoped they would turn around and go back to the coast. Breakfast had been a huge affair, and with Eva's departure, he was feeling sick in the stomach. There was much to fix there, and he wanted to find her and explain.

"Nothing less small-town than the pub?" Stef lounged against the verandah before screeching enough to startle them all. "Oh, my goodness." She was rubbing something off her white blouse; it was mould from the timber rail.

He held a tight grip on a smile while Brittany tutted beside Stef, both vying for ideas on how to remove stains off an expensive-looking blouse.

It was time to make a move. "Come on, you lot. You can lower your standards for one day." He would introduce them to the massive timber-built pub featured in the centre of Malanda and constructed over a hundred years ago. Built of good, solid hardwoods and rich in history, he couldn't believe he was defending the town he once hated with a passion. But then again, it wasn't the town's fault he felt that way.

They grumbled behind him, but he refused to pander to them. Sure, there were some nicer boutique cafés attached to many of the tourist attractions, but the pub was serving him well so far. If they didn't like it, they could leave. They'd caused enough strife for one day.

"I'll need a quick shower first. How about you guys drop by the visitor's centre, and I'll message you when I'm on my way?"

Jack had an urge to move this crowd on and search for Eva. Why? He wasn't so sure. Opening himself up to Eva should scare the hell out of him, but she'd offered to listen to him and strangely, he wanted to talk.

CHAPTER 13

Eva's phone pinged with an incoming message, but she ignored it. It was after nine pm, and if it was work related, it could wait until tomorrow. Again, she concentrated on her book, a hot romance where the hero resembled Jack in too many ways. A steamy sex scene was probably on the cards in the next few pages. She could dream, couldn't she?

When her phone pinged twice more, she huffed and flung the book facedown beside her. She lay snuggled in bed and had given herself the night off. It was permission to wind down and take her mind off everything. Eva stretched her legs and wiggled her toes. On the rare nights she wasn't rushing to get her next edition out, she loved nothing more than her bed, a comfy pillow and a great book. She grinned, realising her thoughts made her sound like a grandma.

Messages this late at night were sometimes from her sister, but she doubted it this time. Her sister and brother-in-law were holidaying in Vietnam for two weeks. If there was some sort of family emergency, her dad or Nan would call.

So why wasn't she snatching the phone from her bedside table and checking it? It wasn't a big deal. Grab it, tap in her password, read the message, take down a note or two for the next day. Job done!

Eva pulled the pillow from under her head, squashed it against her face and groaned. She couldn't fool herself. No word from Jack in three days, and this bothered her. Not because of her damn feelings but because she'd read him so wrong. She had a knack for reading people, but she'd completely messed up this time. *He has a girlfriend? And he kissed me like he had a right to?*

The phone pinged twice more. Eva growled and flung the pillow aside. Reaching across for it, she knocked a framed photo of her mum and dad, and it dropped to the tiled floor. Her heart lurched when it landed face down, the glass shattering.

She rolled onto her stomach, aghast at what she'd done. Shards of glass littered the floor around the frame. Careful not to cut herself, she picked it up and turned it around. It'd been a while since she'd studied the photo of her parents, and she took a moment to look at it again. Too bad her eyes started to tear up. Straightening her pillow, she lay back on it and sniffled.

It was her all-time favourite photo of them. Her father's face was slightly turned on its side, and the look of love reflected all over it as he gazed at her mother always overwhelmed her. Her mother basked in it. Eva always envied the love this photo symbolised. She was so far from experiencing that connection that it was a joke. The family curse would end it all soon anyway, which only caused her tears to flow more freely. It was just her luck. At least it would end with her. She had no daughter to carry it forward.

Needing to get up and sweep away the mess, she reached for the box of tissues first and sat it on her stomach with the frame. With a couple of tissues in hand, she blew her nose and wiped her eyes. What was the big deal? She'd known her thirtieth birthday was the time limit even though no one in the family had ever spoken about it or suggested such a thing.

The phone pinged again, and this time she grabbed it with no further disaster.

Her heart thumped at the messages from Jack.

After lunch with my friends, my fridge arrived.

Friends? Nice try, Jack.

My furniture arrived the next morning. It wasn't much, but it took a few hours to sort out.

So what? Why was he telling her this? She scrolled down to the following message.

Then Mick kidnapped me for two days, and we made a start on the new cabin. It was hard to say no to Jillian's cooking.

Eva smiled at that.

Will you invite me on your next hike?

She's not my girlfriend.

Eva did her best to ignore the tingling over her skin. *Stop it!*

Each line was a separate message, the reason for so many pings earlier. Something her sister often did, especially when she wanted Eva's attention immediately. She wiped one clammy hand down her night shirt and dropped the phone on the tissue box. What sort of response did he want? Was it only a week ago they first met? Should she risk one last fling before her birthday?

The phone pinged again, and she jerked at the sound. *What now?*

I'm sorry.

Eva sagged into her mattress. Her hand shook as she contemplated her reply. The next day she was due at the rescue park, but she planned a hike to the Bones Knob

Lookout on Thursday. The WW2 igloo bunkers built during the war were worthy of some photos, and she would feature them in her Anzac edition in a few months' time. *Maybe.*

Her hand hovered over her phone before she tapped: **Thursday morning, 7 am. I'll pick you up.** Then she pressed send and released the breath she held.

An immediate response came back.

I'll be ready.

Then another ping.

Can't wait.

Eva's skin tingled as she made a move to get off the bed to clean the mess. That steamy sex scene was exactly what she didn't need. Or did she? She swung her legs to the side, careful not to step on the glass, and groaned as she made her way to the broom cupboard. *Is this going to end badly?*

Jack dragged his swag inside the house and dropped it near the front door. He intended to spend a few minutes with Eva's furry family before she turned up. He'd purposely set his alarm early, suspecting Eva hadn't been over to see them recently. Stef's selfish actions would undoubtedly have upset her, and he agonised for days about apologising. If he sold up and left the area, would it be better this way? Guilt had won over in the end.

He dressed in his hiking gear, ran his fingers through his hair to flatten it and washed his face in the bathroom sink. The dim light couldn't hide the stained and splotched marks on the delaminating timber grain vanity top. He couldn't wait to replace it.

Wait. What? He rested both hands on top and stared at his reflection in the mirror. His slack jaw resembled a drunken man. Why would he want to replace it if he didn't intend on staying? And how could he stay? The nightmares reached out to claw at him again last night. By about midnight and in sheer desperation, he dragged the swag out on the verandah and slept fitfully. At least it was something.

Jack sighed and turned away from the mirror. One bed had arrived with his furniture, and he debated which room to assemble it in. There were five to choose from. All small and pokey, but in the end, he put it in the room his mother used for ironing and sewing. It still hadn't helped.

Making his way to the front door, he grabbed his torch, a piece of packing cardboard he left beside his backpack and made his way to the backyard.

At some ungodly hour of the night, when his brain had whirred with too much thinking and the nightmares retreated for a moment, the idea came to him to knock some walls out and change the entire dynamics of the house. This way, he wouldn't recognise his parents' room or which one was his.

Jack stopped midstride on the dewy grass. The familiar pang of panic was still trying to rear its ugly head, and he took a moment to take a deep breath and steady his heart rate. The thought of living this nightmare every night caused a light sheen of sweat to build on his forehead. He huffed and gave himself a mental shake. He'd think about it later. Outside the house, away from the tormenting memories, he had a sense of things returning to normal. Right now, he wanted to check on Eva's family, and he was fast running out of time.

At the usual spot, he placed the cardboard down and plonked himself on it. He closed his eyes, breathed in slowly, then released it, repeating it a couple of times until the adrenalin racing through his veins calmed.

The strong, heady smell of the rainforest worked its

magic on him, and he inhaled it deeply. It settled somewhere comfortably inside, allowing him to lean back against their tree and open his eyes. Light filtered past the canopy, and he immediately spotted about a dozen tree kangaroos. "Hey, guys," he half-whispered in the early quiet, "how have you been?"

There was some movement as roos moved about from branch to branch. Some chewed on leaves, and one cute joey poked his face out of his mother's pouch. A paternal chord jerked as he watched the young joey jiggle about. *These damn animals are growing on me.* He smiled, wishing for all the world that Eva was sitting beside him. He didn't always scowl.

"Hey."

Jack spun around towards the voice, his breath hitching in his throat.

"I wasn't expecting to see you here," Eva said softly. "Since the front door was open, I thought I could sneak in a quick check of my babies."

She carried a yoga mat under her arm, but Jack moved over to the edge of the cardboard and patted the spot beside him. "You haven't been for a few days, have you?"

Eva sat close enough that their arms touched, causing the now familiar frisson, and looked up. "No."

While Eva studied the roos, Jack studied her. How was this one woman worming her way into his well-organised world and threatening to turn it upside down? Like a craving for a cigarette, he wanted more of her. He couldn't explain it. He had a life in Brisbane, a job he loved as a pilot, a bank of investments to rival the entire value of Malanda. Jack didn't need this. He didn't need this headache of a property and a promise made a long time ago to the only person who'd unconditionally loved him—until she left him all alone in this ugly world.

But Eva transformed that ugliness with a single glance and had shown him more beauty in one week than he'd experienced in a lifetime.

"Eva?" he whispered.

She didn't turn around immediately and swallowed. Jack rubbed his fingers against his palm and hoped like hell she turned around soon. His whole body waited on standby like his aircraft did before take-off. He waited for the anticipated adrenalin of reaching for the skies. She didn't disappoint. When she dragged her eyes off her babies and finally looked his way, he soared. In his mind, a clear blue sky arched above them, and the world was right again.

His face moved a fraction, and Eva did the same, leaning closer. When his mouth touched hers, a burst of sun shone through the aircraft window and into the cockpit. He was in his happy place and reaching for the stars. Her warmth spread to his body as he drew her closer and enclosed her in his arms. And just like the other time he kissed her this passionately, it was fucking amazing.

CHAPTER 14

"What's this place called?"

"Bones Knob," Eva replied, endorphins still pumping around her body after their kiss barely an hour ago.

"And we could've driven here? I see we're walking on a perfectly drivable road."

Eva stopped for a moment to catch her breath. They were approaching the summit of the hill, and while it wasn't as strenuous as other walks she'd done, her heart was protesting, wishing it was in sleep mode instead. "Where's the fun in that when you can combine exercise and splendid company all in the one package?" She finished her statement with a big cheesy grin and, for that, Jack rewarded her with one of his precious, brilliant smiles. It was only fleeting, but it caused her heart to skip a beat. "You're the one who nagged me to come on my next hike. I'm just doing a job here."

Jack relaxed and reached across for her hand. His touch sent a current along her arm, and she didn't protest when he gently tugged on it. Her breath snagged somewhere in her throat when he reached in and placed a kiss below her ear.

"So, who's Stef?"

Jack jerked back and scowled. "Ow, way to kill a moment."

Eva had to get it off her chest. "I think Stef killed the moment first. A friend doesn't kiss someone the way Stef did the other day." She had nothing to lose by asking.

"I know, and she got words from me about it. I'm sorry."

She stared hard at him for several seconds. "And? What's the story with you pair?"

Jack puffed out a weary sigh. "Once upon a time, she might've wanted something more. I met her a long time ago when I first arrived in Brisbane. I was working at a café, and I served her and a bunch of her friends their lattes. It—"

"Okay, let's keep going," Eva interrupted. "We're nearly there. It's none of my business, sorry." Eva strode off, angry at herself for prying.

"Hey, didn't you ask for the story?"

"I did," she flung back, "but I shouldn't have."

"Yes, you should have. I'd want to know if it was me watching someone kissing you," Jack declared a few paces behind her.

Eva huffed and spun around. "Why, Jack? What's in it for you?"

"Hey"—Jack raised his hands in surrender—"I'm not sure what's happening here, but if you can't feel something, then you're made of stone." He dropped his hands by his side, and his handsome face sobered. "I feel something, but I'm not sure whether you do, too."

Eva lost the frustrated stance, and her shoulders drooped. "I'm sorry, there's just a lot going on." She shrugged her backpack off and reached across to pull off Jack's.

"What are you doing?" Jack asked as he dropped his to the ground. "Even I can tell we're not at the top yet."

"Shut up and let me give you a hug." Their eyes locked.

Eva wound her arms around his neck, and Jack put his around her waist. "Now squeeze tight," she ordered. Like fusing two pieces of plastic, they melded as one. Eva swallowed against his neck and inhaled everything about Jack. The usual hint of fresh pine from his aftershave and the added dash of sweat from exertion. She wanted to be able to recall it when she was in heaven. And she'd better be going there. If her family history made her leave this earth early, she wanted a spot reserved for her.

"You're different from anyone I've ever met," Jack whispered.

Every pulse point along her body awoke at this declaration. As she squeezed tighter, she realised two things. She had to tell Jack about her curse, and she had to tell him she knew his father. But she didn't want to spoil the moment and needed to hear his version. To tell him the truth of what Harold told her could break him. She had no idea how to broach it.

She pulled back abruptly, seriously confused about what to do. "Let's keep going."

Jack eyed her like he was searching for clues. She kept her face neutral, though it was killing her. He frowned. No surprise there. She took a swig of water before picking up her backpack.

Jack hoisted his bag and slung it over his shoulders. His footsteps fell in line with hers. "What sort of place is this 'Bones Knob'?"

"It has an interesting history and a magnificent view. It involves the war and massacres," Eva answered as they started on the final ascent.

"Great. Sounds like the perfect place to tell my story. Will we have time?"

Eva halted and grabbed Jack's hand as he continued to

walk. He spun around with his signature scowl in place. She asked, "Are you sure?"

Jack nodded. "Walk, Eva. Yes, I'm sure."

She couldn't lie. It was what she was hoping for, but all Eva wanted to do was run her fingers along his frown lines and smooth them out one by one. Talking about his childhood was a big deal for Jack, and he'd chosen her for the job. "I'd like to be back before any possible afternoon storm," she said.

"I thought that would be fun, getting caught up in a storm. We'd be soaking wet and huddled together somewhere and—"

A tremble of the unwanted kind took a grip over Eva and the blood drained from her face. Whatever Jack said after that, she didn't hear for the buzzing in her ears. For reasons unrelated to the exertion of walking up a hill, her breathing laboured in her chest. She bent over, trying to calm the panic itching to take over.

"Hey, are you okay?"

Jack's hand on her shoulder took her mind off the sudden panic attack. When he began rubbing her back in gentle circles, she could breathe deeply and hold it for a few seconds before doing it again. It was enough to quell the attack. She pasted a big fake smile on her face and straightened her back. "All good. This hill must be harder than I remembered."

"*I'm* not puffed," Jack stated, "and you can't fool me that I'm fitter than you."

"Maybe it's a stitch."

Jack continued to scrutinise her. His critical gaze exposed her as a liar, but it was better this way.

"So, ah"—it was time to change the subject—"this place was converted into private property years ago and is currently on the market again."

Jack's face tilted; doubt about whether she was okay was written all over it. "Are we allowed to be here?"

"Yes, but because of its historical value, I needed a council permit."

"So, just you and me alone?"

This time a shiver travelled up along her back, despite the early summer heat beginning to pelt down over them. "Yes, so you better behave." She turned away before he read too much.

Jack scoffed behind her. "Nice try, Eva. I bet you don't know the meaning of the word."

"You don't know me, Jack," she tossed over her shoulder.

"But I want to."

She ignored this and bit into her lip. A small throb threatened the sides of her brow. If she weren't careful, it would explode into an almighty headache. *Calm down, girl.* She wanted Jack to share his story first, and then she'd tell hers—next.

Next week.

Next month.

She held in a groan. She might not have a next month.

Ah, yep. Her fingers kneaded her head through the cap she wore, the curse working its magic by screwing her up.

"Mum could see my anger was growing." Jack straightened against the tree they chose for their picnic. He eyed the banquet Eva provided, and the edges of his mouth turned up a fraction.

"How old were you?"

"Seventeen. I didn't realise it, but the anger was brewing,

and she had to get me out of the place before I did something stupid that couldn't be reversed."

"Like what?" Eva asked as she spread jam on a cracker.

"I wanted to kill him. I still do on some terrible days."

Eva's hand froze and she looked up. "Oh, Jack, that's not a nice place to be."

"Tell me about it. But nothing we did could stop his temper, his violence against Mum, the shouting and punching walls. We were perfectly isolated. He could do what he liked because no one would hear it. By seventeen, he couldn't lock me away in the wardrobe anymore, but I'd lock myself in my room and kick a few walls myself."

Jack sat mesmerised by the V formation of a flock of cranes flying overhead. "I should have done something." If only he'd stood up to the old bastard. He'd never been game enough to leave his mother alone, but on that final day, she insisted.

His mother thrust the bank book at him and told him to go. If he loved her, she said, he would leave and make a life for himself. Jack had argued, but she stood firm. When his father collapsed after another drunken stupor, Jack left. The image of his mother shimmered in his mind. She managed one last smile before he turned away. For days, he hung onto her last smile, but the news of her death had shattered that.

"Did you ever seek any help?"

Eva's intrusion into his thoughts jolted Jack back to the present. He rubbed his fingers over his eyes and gently massaged them. "I tried a few times, but nothing helped. I'm hoping that coming back to face it as an adult might help put it all to rest."

"Sometimes it's not straightforward. I hope for your sake it is."

Jack shrugged off the melancholy his mind conjured and picked up a ham and salad roll. He attempted a smile, but it failed to hold. "So, I came back to the house. I don't give a damn about needing to face my father. He can go to hell for all I care."

Eva's sweet face twisted into a grimace. "Is it helping so far?"

Jack looked out at the spectacular view from where they sat. On the walk up, Eva told him they were looking towards the southern Tablelands, with Bones Knob at the edge of the last lava flow. He tilted his face up and enjoyed the rush of the sun's heat on it. The clear blue sky mocked him. He wanted to be up there in it. "Not yet. I'm still struggling to sleep a night through inside the house."

Eva was close enough to reach across and squeeze his hand. Talking about his father and being raised around violence had a strange effect. Was Eva the right person to tell? Now, facing her calm acceptance of him at his most vulnerable, he knew she was. Change wouldn't happen overnight, but already he was feeling lighter. It was as though his plane had taken off and he was levelling out.

"Tell me more about this place," Jack asked, deciding it was time to change the subject. There wasn't much more to tell about his miserable childhood.

Eva gently disentangled her hand from his and looked out over the escarpment. She raised her knees and rested her arms on top. Jack took this opportunity to keep eating, amazed by how much variety Eva snuck in her backpack. The sweet aroma of mango was enough enticement to push it next on the menu for his ever-grumbling stomach.

"The igloos were built in 1943 by the army to house radar electronics and two-tonne consoles for a transmitter and receiver."

Jack nodded, enjoying the sweet fruit, something that was rare in his diet.

"They intended for the igloos to be earth covered, but it never happened. The Aussie troops were going to use them for training in the final phase of the New Guinea campaign, but I don't think too much happened here. It's since been heritage listed and sold privately. The last owner died a couple of years ago, and they discovered a trove of her artwork inside one of the igloos. Her only family lived in Germany, and they had no idea of her art collection."

Jack crunched on a grape, enjoying the sound of Eva's voice in the stillness of the surrounding nature.

"Historians also claim it was the sight of an Aboriginal massacre. They were killed and thrown over this very edge."

A shudder rolled along Jack's shoulders. It was too easy to kill if a person was provoked enough. He remembered those thoughts all too well. What if he'd exploded and done the inevitable? How might his life have panned out?

Used to pushing troubling thoughts to the back of his mind, Jack conjured up a smile and turned in Eva's direction. "Thanks for this history lesson, and … thanks for listening."

Her arms fell away from her knees, and a thoughtful expression crossed her face. "I hope it helps in some small way."

"It already has. Also, thanks for all this great food. You're amazing."

Eva shrugged nonchalantly before her trademark smile stretched across her face and did all sorts of things inside his body. She plopped a piece of mango in her mouth and said, "You eat anything. It's no trouble at all."

Jack stared at Eva like a happy dog, basking in the glow of being close to her. Honestly, it didn't take much. "Is the offer still on to help me buy a few basics for the house?"

A smidgen of anxiety hovered across her features for a second. "I have all the photos I need, so let's pack up this party and head back. We have plenty of time to fit in some shopping."

"Did you make that list?" Jack asked, pressing lids to containers and passing them to Eva.

"Nope, wasn't in the mood."

He knew better than to ask why.

"But if you offer to drive into Atherton, I'll have it done before we get there," she added.

Of course she would. This was Eva who could complete a thousand chores in one day. What was a list? Jack had *one* chore to do, and momentarily scowling, he realised he had a lot of work ahead of him before completing it. But manage it, he would, one day at a time. He sent Eva a grateful smile. "Deal."

Step one was to get a handle on his past and make it through the night without waking up in a sweat. Talking to Eva opened a channel where all things seemed possible again. Regardless of what happened to the property, he was determined to rid himself of the nightmares and progress from one step to the next. He just wasn't sure what step two was yet.

He handed over the last container. While Eva packed it into her bag, he reached across and gave her a quick peck on her cheek. Any more than that and they'd never leave this place in a hurry. She fumbled with the zipper of her backpack, so he took over. When he handed it back, a slight blush covered her cheeks. She looked adorable. A word he hadn't used to describe a woman in a long time.

They both rose while Jack rolled up the mat. Packing it away in his bag, he was already feeling confident about a lot of things.

CHAPTER 15

"Follow me, Jack." Eva pointed to a path leading into the forest.

"Back in there, huh?"

"Ah, yup." She smiled at Jack's confusion like it was some top-secret mission they were on.

In the three days since their shopping expedition, they hadn't seen each other. Jack was kept busy at Mick's place while she'd longed for his company. It was time to get her mind off what she'd really love to do in the dark forest once they were alone. "How's Mick's cabin coming along?" she asked, gently treading over the undergrowth leading away from the roo park.

"Really well. A few more days of work to go." Jack patted his stomach when she glanced back at him. "I better watch my figure around Jillian's cooking, though."

Eva smiled at the absurdity of his comment. Jack's physique was perfectly proportioned. He was a head taller and had biceps that had her licking her dry lips. Not to mention the washboard abs she witnessed on top of Windin Falls.

She swallowed. Just thinking about what lay beneath his shirt had her longing for it. "Well, er, Mick seems to manage."

"Yes, but Mick is on the go all day long. He has the farm, the B & B and the kids. In a few weeks, there will be an extra one. He'll need all the energy he can get."

Eva stopped suddenly, remembering what they were supposed to be doing. "Ah, sorry," she said when Jack stumbled behind her, his hand falling on her hip.

"What are we looking for?" Jack asked.

Jack's warm breath tickled her neck, and she pinched her eyes closed, wanting more than anything to turn around and kiss him. She was a wreck because she hadn't seen Jack for a few days. Her nights had turned sleepless. Trying to fall asleep was impossible. All she thought about were Jack's blue eyes and chiselled jawline, and that mouth, of course. It was a joke. Now, *she* struggled to sleep at night without waking up in a sweat.

Asking if he wanted to volunteer for an afternoon at the roo park had been pure desperation. "We're going to collect leaves from the Privet and Umbrella Trees."

"Hey," Jack spoke quietly near her ear, "as much as I love Mick's company and the amazing food, I missed you."

She sagged against Jack's chest; his arms slipped around her waist.

"I now have a sort of functional home. The internet's connected, and I've got a fridge full of food." His lips grazed that sensitive spot behind her ear. "I'd like to invite you over for dinner."

She cleared her throat, and in between puffs of struggling breaths, she scraped a few words out. "Wh … what's on the menu?"

"This first." Jack turned her around by the shoulders and

leant down to reach her mouth. Dappled shadows played across Jack's face as he inched closer. His tantalising fresh pine scent made her head spin. When his mouth touched hers, the world closed in around them. She was getting distracted every day by Jack and knew it was wrong to instigate something when her time was running out.

She should care. But at that moment, she didn't.

The kiss started tame. Then his tongue darted around her mouth, and when his hands tightened around her waist, it turned sensual and heated. The slow movement of his hands over her back sent a seductive pulse racing around her body. His growing erection pushed against her stomach, and just when she longed for more, for the chance to go one step further, Jack pulled back a fraction and cupped her face.

Her chest heaved as she looked deep into Jack's eyes, worried her unsteady legs might not hold her up for much longer. With Jack's breathing sounding harsh in the quiet of the forest, all she could think of was sinking onto the forest floor and letting him take her to that special place. It'd been so damn long since she'd allowed another man to take her there.

A shaft of light touched the top half of his face. Without breaking the connection, his hands moved slowly down both sides of her neck, over her shoulders and nudged her breasts before tightening around her middle. Why didn't she get on with it and move it along faster? She could convince herself it would be a nice memory for him to have.

"Are baked beans on toast enough of an enticement?"

Eva moaned, hating that he broke the spell. She took a huge gulp of air, trying to steady her heart. "Is that the best you can offer?"

Jack smiled one of his rare million-dollar smiles, and a

tremor shot past her breast. "I would hire Jillian for the night if she wasn't likely to go into labour any day."

Eva shook her head before resting it against Jack's chest. She needed a moment to gather her thoughts and match them with words. She'd had enough of wasting time she didn't have. "We'll manage on baked beans and toast. I'd rather it was just us. Alone," she muffled against his chest.

Jack took a sudden step back, and a startled whimper escaped her mouth. "Eva?"

She raised her face sheepishly and looked at him. Neither moved as Jack processed her offer. She didn't breathe for a few beats.

"Are you sure?"

She couldn't take his probing glance anymore. Disentangling her arms from his firm hold, she wound them around his neck. Pushing to tippy-toes, she whispered near his ear, "I am." The reactive jerk from Jack's body set her alight and left her dizzy with possibilities. She smiled against his neck. "But we have a job to do first. Think you can manage it?"

"Very poorly, if I have to be honest," Jack murmured back. "My mind won't be on the job, that's for sure."

This was true. Neither would *her* mind be on the roo park duties to get through that afternoon. She chuckled softly as Jack's arms tightened around her, believing she'd made the right decision. Maybe she could help Jack create new memories in his childhood home. Her wish would be for Jack to keep the house and the forest intact for her babies. For Jack, she wished him lots of love and happiness. With a heavy heart and a great deal of pity, she wouldn't be around to witness it.

Jack's arms were loaded with leaves from the Privet and
Umbrella Trees, and their freshly picked fragrance floated
up to his nose. The aromatic smell reminded him of how
vibrant and alive the forest was and how this was rubbing
off on him in a good way. Was he the same man who'd
fallen into a depressive hole only weeks ago? Spending time
with Mick and his family, and Eva, was helping him heal in
a way he'd never considered possible when he'd decided to
return.

Little ants and other insects scurried over his arms, their
biting pinpricks not enough to halt their chores. *Get the job
done, fast.*

Every glance at Eva and every touch heightened the
anticipation of what she promised could happen later. He
shook his head and tucked away the thoughts for now. He
needed to listen to what Eva was saying. She finished
explaining why they chose the Privet and Umbrella Trees
leaves. That they were readily available was fair enough.
Then she listed the chores they had to do, which sounded
longer than his arm. It would take forever before they could
get away.

Still, he watched Eva with awe. Her ability to get so much
done in a day astounded him. If she was thinking about what
might happen that night, it certainly didn't show. Her work
didn't falter, and her conversation didn't either for the entire
time they spent collecting leaves. In another time and place,
he might've been bored, but she was a wealth of information
to rival Dr Karen's and made it all sound fascinating.

When Eva decided they'd collected enough, they made
their way back to the roo park. His mouth turned dry as he
struggled to drag his gaze away from the hypnotic swing of
her hips in khaki pants. The thought of touching those hips
left him jittery and impatient. How many hours until dinner?

He almost let out a groan to echo under the dense canopy but clamped down on his jaw instead.

Back at the roo park, the sheltered forest concealed the summer afternoon. It didn't look like a storm was building up, but that only meant there'd be no reprieve from the stifling heat. Jack dropped the bundle of leaves on a make-shift table and lifted his loose cotton shirt to swipe across his brow.

"Here, put this on."

Eva thrust a large straw hat in his direction, and he shoved it on. It might make him sweat more, but it would save him from getting burnt. He would bring his own next time. Then he flicked some crawling insects off his arm before beginning the long list of chores Eva had recited in the forest.

First, they'd remove any old leaves and uneaten food from the tray boxes. Eva directed him with a touch here and enough eye contact to reinforce how easy it was for him to work up a sweat in her presence. He couldn't blame the afternoon sun for all of it. Then the cages required cleaning with the sand changed in the tray bottoms. With around two dozen cages, this was no mean feat. Fresh dishes of water to be refilled in each cage along with the extra food. On today's menu, the tree kangaroos would get chickpeas, sweet potato and bananas. It needed to be cut up and put into clean trays.

"How often do you do this every week?" Jack asked Eva as they worked companionably with a couple of extra volunteers.

Eva smiled back before reaching up to his cheek for the briefest of kisses. That little trick almost blew him away. Maybe she *was* thinking about later. The others were turned away, but she blushed adorably before getting back to the chores required.

"Twice a week, sometimes I squeeze in a third day if the volunteers on hand are thin."

"How do you fit everything in?" Jack wanted to know.

"Easy. I get up and do what needs to be done and keep at it until I drop off to sleep at night. Every minute spent here is worth it a thousand times over. I love these furry little bundles and I want to do everything possible to ensure they never disappear from the earth. That's enough motivation to fit this in with everything else I have to do."

Jack momentarily froze. There it was again. The pressures to get his shit sorted and decide what to do with the property. Eva would never forgive him if he sold it to someone who didn't show any interest in the kangaroos. What sort of train wreck was he heading into if things happened later that night? Would it leave him in a corner with no way of getting out?

Eva left his side and went to prepare formula milk for the little ones. Even for a few minutes, her absence had his chest hollowing out. Holding off for three days nearly killed him, but he had no reason to contact her. Well, nothing valid that didn't come across as desperate. Her invitation to help volunteer had left him shaking with relief, which was something new in his books.

For now, he mumbled inane words quietly, getting back to the chore of chopping bananas. He was tempted to sneak in a couple of pieces. The fruity smell had been tantalising his nose for the past ten minutes, and the usual grumbles of his stomach had already started. How the hell was baked beans on toast going to fix that?

Frowning, he debated whether he should pick up some fish and chips from the local café. He hadn't thought this out at all, and his lame meal suggestion had come out in a rush. Sighing, he dropped his shoulders. All the while his hands were on autopilot as he peeled another banana before chopping it up into neat pieces.

When Eva returned, she brushed her arm against his, and he jolted at her touch. "You can give me a hand feeding the babies. They will finish the food prep."

She referred to the other volunteers, so he put his knife down and followed Eva without a murmur. He would follow her to the ends of the earth if she asked. Should he be concerned? He shook his head. He had no idea why everything about Eva felt right. "Dr Karen's not around today?"

"She's at a council meeting trying to drum up support for more funding."

He rather hoped Dr Karen would show up sometime that afternoon. Her vast depth of information was interesting, and he was curious about what else they could do to research their blindness. An anonymous donation spent wisely could go a long way. It was an idea he'd been mulling over since his last visit.

"I'll get you Tommy again. Take a seat, same as last time." Within a minute, Jack had Tommy on his lap with the same slurping tugs sucking out the formula. Eva sat on the other chair, close enough that Jack moved his thigh to touch hers. She looked up and Jack dropped his face and found her mouth. He ended the chaste kiss by grabbing her bottom lip between his teeth and giving it the gentlest of bites.

It was enough to make her gasp and nearly drop the furry bundle. Jack came away quickly and shot his arm out to save the baby roo from falling to the ground. Eva's surprise reaction had him chuckling. Once they settled the baby roo again, the bottle was empty in no time.

Eva rose and tugged the bottle away from the roo's mouth and shoved it in her side khaki pocket. "How's Tommy going?" She fidgeted with the rug around the tree roo and sounded flustered.

An airy suck signalled Tommy had finished his formula too. These babies were stronger and getting through their drink faster than the last time he'd been there. Jack gently pulled the bottle out of Tommy's mouth and stood. "I wish I was just finishing my dinner."

"Jack!"

A delightful shade of pink flushed her face, and she raised her free hand to cup her heated cheek.

"What?"

"I'm nervous, even if it was my idea."

Relief coursed through his veins. So, she was human, after all, and not the only one distracted by the promise of later. "Just goes to show how fearless you are. I've never been brave enough to make the first move." Jack sauntered off towards Tommy's cage, leaving Eva to follow.

"Liar," she called behind his back.

He chuckled while he waited for her. Eva kept her gaze averted as she put her furry animal back in one cage and then reached across for Tommy and placed him in the cage beside it.

"Next baby, please, so we can get this show on the road," Jack said, producing a mischievous smile.

Eva groaned as she moved along to the next cage. When she passed him the next roo, her touch sent a trail of sensitive tremors along his skin. He managed another innocent kiss, but keeping his hands and mouth off her was proving to be very difficult.

CHAPTER 16

"You were never going to let me order in fish and chips, were you?"

Eva relished the feel of Jack's fingers entwined with hers. Her other hand carried a torch as they entered the dark forest while Jack held the yoga mat tucked under his other arm. "Not when, in half an hour and a few ingredients, you can dish up a delicious plate of pasta."

"But hmm … I invited you to dinner."

Eva chuckled. "Yeah, and I invited myself to your kitchen. Your stomach grumbled way too many times this afternoon."

Jack groaned and squeezed her hand. "My stomach has a mind of its own."

"And baked beans on toast was never going to cut it. Anyway, it gave you another chance to improve your salad-making skills."

"Are you saying my first attempt was lousy?"

Eva chuckled and squeezed him back. "Let's just say practice makes perfect."

"That bad, hey?"

Smiling, she looked across when Jack slowed his steps. "Actions tell a thousand words."

Jack tugged on her hand, forcing her to stop. She turned to face him and her breath hitched.

"But you prefer words, don't you?"

The torch illuminated the spot where they stood, and she looked into his night-time eyes. She fell into those deep pools and enjoyed how desire travelled south and made her head spin. The spark she'd been waiting for all her life was right there between them. She was in her prime and resented how destiny had other plans. She blinked a couple of times and swallowed. She would not shed a single tear, not yet. Her voice came out in a thin whisper, almost too afraid to speak. "No, I think I like actions better."

Jack frowned. Did her expression set off alarm bells? She cast aside the worry. When Jack's mouth dropped, she rose on her toes to meet it. With grim determination, she would live every day like it was her last.

Starting that night.

There would be no holding back and no second thoughts. As Jack's tongue took a slow and sensuous journey, Eva relaxed. She pushed aside thoughts of anything but his mouth and tongue delving deeper. She had to clench her torch-holding hand to a fistful of his shirt.

When Jack pulled back, he ploughed a hand through his hair. She released her grip on his shirt, and when she held the torch up, a hint of his broodiness showed on his face.

"Your babies, we better keep going."

His chest heaved in time with hers, but Eva smiled before placing a quick peck on his cheek. She got that this look was a default setting for him. The result of too many years holding in his past. "Yes, my babies. I haven't seen them for a few days."

"Well, come on." Jack tightened his hold and headed toward her family. "Let's do this."

"Like it's my fault we stopped along the way." Eva giggled, the night forest surrounding them like a comforter.

When he looked across, the torchlight showed a slight relaxing of his frown. "You're a distraction, so technically, yes."

Eva's chest expanded to bursting point. Yep, they were both feeling something. It was reassuring to know it wasn't one-sided.

At the spot, Jack unrolled the mat onto the uneven forest floor. A quick glance up and Eva was relieved her family had settled in for the night. The bright beam from the torch started some rustling, but she shut it down and nestled between Jack's legs with her back against his chest.

When his thighs tightened around her hips, she breathed in deeply. She always felt safe at this spot, day or night, and made an effort to silence her constant chatter for a few minutes. With her hands resting on Jack's legs, she soaked up the ambience of the forest sounds and smells and let contentment settle between them. "I love how it's always so calming here." She whispered into the quiet night, all the while trying to ignore the way her pulse continued to thrum through her body.

Jack grunted and rested his chin on the top of her head. "Except I don't want calm," he countered thickly.

His reply sent an unashamed hunger roaring through her, and a tremor shook at his admission.

Jack's arms tightened. "Hey, are you cold?" His warm breath tickled her neck when his mouth moved gently over it.

Eva moaned, closing her eyes. "No, not at all."

"Good. Now, have you had enough of calm out here?"

Eva snorted and began chuckling.

"Oh, no you don't, Eva. No noise, remember."

"It's not my fault."

"So, technically, it's mine, is it?"

Eva started laughing, the kind that threatened to become uncontrollable.

"Shush, Eva, you'll wake them."

Instead, she laughed harder and could barely stand when Jack rose and pulled her up. He shoved the mat under his arm, grabbed the torch she held, and only managed to keep his mirth in until halfway back.

At the house, they landed roughly on his swag left inside the front door and didn't leave it for the rest of the night.

A curlew's call was the first thing to rouse Jack. The second was the dull hint of sunlight coming through the open front door. There was enough light to study Eva's outline. She slept on her side facing him, her long eyelashes resting gently on her face. The swag was pulled up to her chest, and its outline moved in time with her breathing.

The third thing to catalogue in his foggy head was that he'd slept through the night without waking up once. Suddenly, he was alert and tense, grappling with what this meant. Panic had temporarily crowded his head when they'd arrived back at the house, but he'd made a Herculean effort to push it aside and concentrate on Eva. Nothing else could penetrate after that, and his body stirred afresh at the memory.

It wasn't just the experience of sex she offered him. On his usual scale, it'd burnt a hole off the page somewhere in the ether. Probably at the same height he flew his aircraft. It was more than that. It was her laughter, her chatter, the whole

Eva package. He'd never laughed so much when making love with someone. Had never felt the freedom to add his absurd jokes to the scene. It was a sixth sense telling him that everything he did was pleasing her.

They clicked, they laughed, they talked, they touched, and they loved. Only at the end, when their climax hovered, had the laughter and chatter died down, the rough playfulness settled back and the serious stuff of setting off sparks had taken over. And what a moment it was. His skin tingled in the cool morning air, and a compulsion he couldn't hold back had him feathering his fingertips down her cheek.

Eva mumbled in her half-sleep until, gradually, her eyes opened. She stretched her legs, and when they brushed along his, the electricity spun through his body.

"Morning," she whispered.

"Come here," Jack suggested in a thick voice, his arms opening for her.

Eva wiggled closer to this side and wound her arms around his neck. "How long have you been awake? Did you sleep?"

"Five minutes and yes."

She squeezed tighter. She understood his trauma with the house. It proved nothing until he could manage it on his own, but this was a start, even if it meant Eva had to sleep here every night. He smiled into her hair at the thought.

"You're smiling, Jack."

"Jeez, can't a man have any privacy?"

"You look cuter when you smile."

Jack pulled back. All the forces in the world couldn't stop the smile plastered over his face. There it was again—the start of more banter, jokes and laughter.

For the next little while, he wanted to wipe both their

smiles away. He reached for her naked backside and pulled her closer.

"What if you get visitors?" Eva asked as her breath hitched in her throat. "We left the front door open."

His erection was already stretched enough to nudge against her stomach, and it was time to locate the foil packages he'd carelessly dropped near the head of the swag.

"Hopefully, they'll turn away when they reach the steps." He reached up and patted his hand along the floorboards with no luck.

"We should put up a no flash photography sign. Unless they're only here to take snaps of the swag. This is one almighty asset. It's more comfortable than my bed."

Jack chuckled and scrambled to his knees, continuing his search. "Shush, woman, I have important business to do here."

Eva laughed, watching him with amusement.

"How much did it set you back? I've seen nothing like it."

Jack grumbled, "A few dollars." It had cost more than what Jack wanted to admit. Vexed that he couldn't find what he was looking for, he spotted her torch and stood. *They have to be here somewhere.*

"Wow, thanks for the morning show."

"What?" Jack turned towards a beaming Eva, and the light sparkled on something she was holding aloft. He turned the torch off and fell to his knees. She held the foil package. "How long have you been holding that?"

She giggled. "Long enough to enjoy all *that*."

He groaned playfully, whipping the swag's top cover off and taking his fill of her gloriously naked body. "Two can play this game."

"Oh, yes, please," she begged, biting her bottom lip.

When he wiped the smile from her face, the laughter and banter, he knew she meant business. So did he.

She moaned when his mouth touched hers and squirmed beneath him when he settled over her. When desire struck his core so hard it left him short of breath, she hastily tore the foil package herself, fitted it and begged him to enter. Only then was it safe to relax a smidgen and take them both to that place that left him reeling.

It happened fast and left them panting in each other's arms as dawn edged a little closer. He needed this woman. How he was going to get his life together and fit her and this place in it, he had no idea yet. He'd work on it one day at a time. This was his last thought as he slipped again into a peaceful sleep.

CHAPTER 17

Eva stretched her arms as her phone alarm sounded. "Shit." It was Sunday morning, and she needed to get going. Jack weighed heavily across her chest, but she didn't have time to ease him. "Jack, wake up; I have to go."

Jack mumbled something, but her words only prompted him to tighten his hold. His hands were suddenly everywhere. If Eva didn't shut her mind to how they woke everything inside of her and leave soon, she'd never get to the Triathlon. As the designated photographer and a volunteer, she didn't need to be there at dawn, but they expected her to show up.

Normally, not a problem.

This morning it was.

Then Jack's mouth was everywhere, and she stopped the struggle to enjoy it. "Jack, listen to me."

"I am. Your body is speaking a thousand words a second, and it's not coming out of your mouth."

Eva smiled against his hair. "Jack, I have to go. I'm expected at the lake this morning."

Jack released her, and his hands stopped moving. The only part of his body still moving and expanding was nudging its way nicely against her thigh. "But it's Sunday," he protested.

"I know, triathlon day."

His face popped up with a frown secured to it. "What about breakfast?"

Eva made a colossal effort to disentangle his arms from hers when all she wanted to do was sink into the plush comfort of the swag with him. She also smiled. She loved his frown as much as she loved his smile. It was all part of the Jack she wanted. "You can make it for me and bring it out. I still have to go home, change and grab my camera and gear."

"Huh? Make it for you?"

"Yeah, that baked beans on toast you promised. Some scrambled eggs wouldn't go astray either."

Jack groaned and rolled off her, releasing her to the crisp morning air. She checked the time on her phone; it was now a few minutes past 6.30 am.

"Yeah, I know, criminal isn't it."

"What is?" Eva asked as she rose and searched for her discarded clothes scattered everywhere.

"Getting up at this ungodly hour and on a Sunday morning, when I had so much planned for us at this very spot."

"I bet you did," she said with raised eyebrows while trying to stifle a giggle as she slipped into her knickers and pants. "In this town, you have to share me with the townsfolk."

"It's only hitting home now," Jack complained, sitting up and mussing his morning hair.

"What were your plans for today?" Eva asked as she straightened her clothes, located her keys and purse, and dropped to her knees beside Jack. She wanted one last kiss before leaving.

"You can ask that after last night?"

Eva smiled at his grumpiness, and her heart expanded a little further. "Kiss me, Jack. I need it to get me through the day."

"Your risk if I don't let you out the front door."

"You left it open. I'll make a dash for it before you can stop me."

He cupped her face, and with a forlorn expression, he said, "God, woman, what are you doing to me?"

Eva swallowed roughly, and her chest tightened. A wall of guilt smashed over her. She closed her eyes, hoping to push it away.

"You okay?" he asked.

She squeezed her eyes tighter. How the heck did he sense so much coming from her? "Just kiss me, Jack. Now! Fast!"

Jack growled, deep and throaty, before his mouth touched hers with enough chemistry and electrical currents to burn her to the ground before her thirtieth birthday. She savoured his touch, drew in his essence, inhaled his morning fragrance, and hoped she could at least take that with her.

Eva pulled back reluctantly. Was it so wrong to feel this way? With difficulty, she swallowed back the building emotions threatening to burst. All the while, Jack's thumb drew slow, maddening circles along her jaw and looked at her with his signature frown. He knew something was off.

"What's wrong?"

She flinched, cursing the one rogue tear trickling down her cheek.

"Hey, this is just the start, isn't it? We're not over yet, are we? There isn't someone else I need to know about?"

Eva stumbled to her feet and swiped her face with her arm. She managed a sorry attempt at a half-laugh and grimace wrapped into one. "Sorry, ignore me, and no, there's no one else." *Your only enemy is time*, she wanted to curse, but she didn't even have time to do that. "I need to go," she said as she headed out the front door.

Jack rose and quickly pulled on his shorts. "Is the triathlon at Tinaroo Dam?" he asked, following her outside.

"Yeah, near the boat ramp."

"Okay, I'll be there in an hour with your breakfast, and then I promised Mick another couple of days to finish the cabin."

Eva nodded, opened her ute door, and got in.

"Can I send you progress shots?" Jack asked.

Eva fumbled with the key. This was what she'd been hoping for. For them to be comfortable enough to message all day. She turned the ignition and nodded at the same time. If she was determined to live every moment to the fullest, she needed to start now. Maybe drop some of her volunteering commitments so she could spend more time with Jack.

The noise of the engine rumbled through the quiet front yard. She shoved the gears into reverse and was about to leave when Jack said, "Jillian offered me the spare bedroom tonight so that we can get an early start tomorrow morning." He fidgeted with the hem of his shorts. "Can ... can I see you again?"

Oh, bloody hell! She was already hurting him. How much worse would it be when she wasn't around? He sounded unsure, like he was almost a little afraid she'd reject him. She put the ute back into neutral and strengthened her resolve. *Live every minute like it's your last.* She swung the ute door open, causing Jack to jump out of the way, and got out. Within seconds, she had her arms around his neck in a stranglehold. "Yes, Jack, to everything."

He reciprocated the hug with his arms plastered around her waist. The short hairs on his chest tickled her face. She grabbed another lungful of the smell of his skin, which hinted at their lovemaking. She groaned out her frustrations at not being able to stay for the rest of the day.

Jack nudged her away. "Go!" he demanded, turning her around.

"Yeah, I better," she replied, hopping back into the ute.

Halfway down the driveway, she burst into tears—big, noisy ones with the occasional hiccup. The sort of crying that would leave her face red and blotchy and take a good half hour to disappear—and not give herself away when Jack turned up with her breakfast.

Jack turned away from the retreating ute and climbed the verandah steps. Eva's departure had cast the world in a dull, hazy light. Gone was her laughter, her smile, and the unstoppable energy she carried everywhere with her.

He made his way back inside the house and flopped down onto the comfy swag, folding his arms behind his head. He closed his eyes to the pockmarked walls and the reminders of the hell that was his past. Instead, he brought up images of Eva and their night together. Eva wouldn't believe it, but he was smiling *and* in this house.

He rolled to his side and hugged his pillow. Opening one eye, his gaze landed on the wardrobe. *Shit!* Its removal was still on his list of must-do chores. He might ask Eva for the loan of her ute. Dwelling on it was all it took to start the tightening in his chest as a mild panic attack wove its way through him.

Spotting the discarded yoga mat, he jumped up, snatching it and his carelessly flung shirt from the night before, and stormed outside. He couldn't have it both ways. He couldn't have Eva *and* the house if he didn't have the strength to remain inside its walls. Back on the verandah, he stretched the shirt over his head and pushed his feet into joggers. He had a few minutes before needing to make the promised breakfast, and Eva's babies had calmed him before. Stupid, he knew, but that favourite spot of Eva's was probably saving his life.

He found the energy to push aside the tingling panic sensation and made his way to the backyard. Breathing in and breathing out. Slowly, carefully, while watching his footing after he passed into the dense canopy of the forest.

Whoever said living in a rural and remote area was peaceful was a liar. The forest was alive with the noises of birds and the scurrying of animals underfoot. He could smile again now that his heart had calmed and his breathing was normal. He'd never get a decent sleep-in with that racket outside a bedroom window.

When he reached the family of roos, he spread out the mat and leant back against *their* favourite tree. When he looked up, he was relieved the roos were going about their business. That was all he needed. His shoulders sagged, and the tension left his body. He could do this.

With Eva's help and her torrent of energy, he made the first resolution he'd made in a long time. As soon as he finished helping Mick, he would get rid of the wardrobe and knock out some walls. Baby steps, but he had to work out for himself if the house was a place he could live in. Part-time, at least.

A frown tightened his brow. He had his Brisbane home and his other life. Meshing it together with a life this far north was a problem for another day. *Baby steps*, he reminded himself. He'd given himself a year; surely, some solution would eventuate in that time.

Now for breakfast. He spotted the baby joey poking its face out of its mother's pouch as he got to his feet and rolled up the mat. He deemed it his good luck detector. Never one to dally with superstitious rot, this thought surprised him. With his breathing under control, he would storm back inside the house and head straight for the kitchen. He'd never made breakfast for anyone, but Eva was turning out to be a surprise first on many counts. Toast, baked beans and some scrambled eggs. How hard could it be? Throw together an overnight bag for Mick's place and the day would be over before he knew it.

There was no time to dwell on anything, which was a new experience. *Thank you, Eva,* he mouthed, giving her babies one last glance before leaving. If Eva taught him anything, it was the value of keeping busy all day. He'd never looked at life that way before.

CHAPTER 18

Eva flicked through the photos on her phone of Mick's new cabin and smiled at the funny antics of both Mick and Jack. She gulped down her breakfast, hurrying to get back to her latest *What's Up* edition. She struggled to concentrate on it and was working dangerously close to her deadline. This was never a good place to be.

In another shot, Jack carried young Trevor on his shoulders while Trevor wielded a kids-sized hammer. Eva sighed. She needed to put the phone down and edit the triathlon photos.

Before she did, she re-read the message Jack sent after the images.

After today, Mick won't need me for a couple of weeks. He's waiting on the plumbing and electrical work to be done and the glaziers to install the windows and doors. I'll be back home tonight.

Something in her chest tightened. Was this an invitation? God, she hoped so. She hadn't seen him since her eggs-on-toast breakfast two days ago, and her ability to focus had gone out the window. She caught herself daydreaming a hundred times a day ever since. Not to mention cursing about how much time she and Jack were wasting by being apart. It left her resentful and depressed about how close her birthday was.

She pushed her empty breakfast plate away and sighed again. With so little time left, she could just throw the towel in and give up. But it wasn't her way. She'd devote her days to her work and passions right until the last minute, just in case history got it all wrong and she was somehow spared, which reminded her that the next afternoon at the roo park was the designated volunteer day for the residents of the aged-care facility. No doubt Harold would ask about the promised update on Jack. She swallowed, nervous about what to tell him. *Ah, I've fallen for your son; we had the most amazing sex, and I want to do it again and again.*

Better not. Rubbing her arm, she worried about the state of her mind. She double-checked the time Jack sent the message and noted it was about an hour ago. It was probably while he was having breakfast after the milking.

She flicked through her own gallery and found the photo she'd taken of Jack looking up at the green tree frog. It was now officially one of her favourites. She attached it and added it to his last message.

Thought I'd include this one in my next edition. You okay with that?

She was about to switch off her phone and knuckle down when it pinged in the quiet of her kitchen. Her heart sped up.

The frog looks great.

Her phone pinged again.

If you must.

Eva smiled. This was consent enough. Another ping.

Will I see you tonight?

She groaned and dropped her face into her hands. If she

hadn't wasted so much time over the past two days, she'd have her latest magazine ready for printing. She lifted her face and reached for the phone again.

I'm running behind with my mag.

Eva tapped furiously.

Struggling to concentrate on it. Technically, your fault.

She received a smiling emoji and imagined his smug grin at the other end.

Must have it ready by lunch tomorrow. Then I'm on at the roo park for the afternoon.

This time she received a sad-face emoji.

I'm free the next night.

Six excited-face emojis appeared and a red heart. The air whooshed out of her lungs. She'd thought of nothing else since their incredible night together.

The phone pinged with his next message.

I've missed you.

She groaned even louder in her quiet kitchen. She *had* to get back to work and concentrate.

Me too. But I need to get back to work.

Three dots bubbled on the screen for half a minute.

Ok, me too. Just finishing an early smoko.

She closed the conversation, took her empty plate to the sink and vowed she wouldn't look at her phone again until after dinner. Could she hold that pledge? Would the lure of more conversation with Jack be too much?

She left the kitchen, pulling her hair into a messy bun. In her office, she locked the door, determined to get the job done. She wasn't coming out until the magazine was ready to send to the printers.

Come on, girl, no one has ever distracted you like this before.

Then again, Jack wasn't just anyone.

Jack eyed the shrivelled rubber plug and hoped it would hold water. He was more surprised it was still around. He'd hosed the old, concrete-style laundry tub with the remnants of a hose he found coiled up underneath the house. His next shopping list would include a new washing machine to be delivered and a hose from the local hardware shop.

A new washing machine? Did this suggest permanency?

He closed his gaping mouth and filled the now not-so-mouldy laundry tub. Jillian had done one load of his washing, but the clothes he wore stank of cattle dung and sweat. They needed an urgent soaking, and without a washing machine and no desire to drive into town to use the laundromat, he'd get his hands dirty by doing it the way he remembered his mother sometimes did.

This memory was enough for Jack to grimace in the privacy of his backyard. His mother had done it tough. For a well-to-do young woman whose well-respected father worked many years in the local council, she'd fallen in love with a boy from the wrong side of town.

As to which town his father came from, he didn't think he'd ever been told. Did his mother ever learn who the man she married really was? Jack had a vague recollection of his mother arguing with his grandfather over Harold's ability to hold down a job. Jack was young, but he didn't doubt his grandfather had died a broken and disappointed man over his daughter's choice of husband.

Leaving his clothes to soak, he made a concerted effort to change the direction his thoughts were headed. It would only leave him glum. He'd had a great couple of days. In the years since spending time with Mick's family, nothing had changed. Mick was still on the 'normal indicator' of how a family should live. They chatted about many things while the cabin slowly transformed into shape. The only subject they never touched on was his father. Mick knew better.

Jack itched to annoy Eva with more messages but ruled it out. He understood the work commitment and had some catching up to do that night with his investments.

Instead, he took slow, measured steps around the house and let ideas filter through his mind. The back of the house could feature a patio. It would be the perfect place to eat breakfast while he watched the kookaburras and curlews enjoy their own. Stimulating smells from the forest would welcome him each morning and fill him with heady scents.

There was room enough to include a double carport, hidden but tacked onto one side. It was a good idea to keep the vehicles out of the weather and yard, where a snake wasn't enticed to curl up near a warm radiator. He'd seen that once as a kid.

An hour later and crammed with ideas, Jack rushed inside and switched on his laptop. He'd dabbled in building designs before, and this was no different. Start with the basic layout and work around it with new ideas.

A couple of hours later, he couldn't ignore the grumble of his stomach. Jack quickly ingested a toasted cheese sandwich for dinner and then another one, his mind far too alert to put the project aside. He justified his lack of cooking skills by how spoilt he'd been over the past few days. Between Eva and Jillian, he was confident he'd eaten enough nutrients to get through at least one night.

A smile tugged at the corner of his lips, and his thoughts returned to the room layout he wanted inside the house, including the additional office he planned to tack onto the weatherboard side. Ideal for his work commitments, or maybe the production of a monthly magazine? Baby Nursery?

His fingers froze over the keys when he questioned the path his thoughts had taken. The lingering smell of melted cheese in the air interrupted his thoughts, and he decided he could go another round of toasted sandwiches. Until he registered the time was three am, and he could barely manage an exhausted smile. It was funny how the mind worked when you pushed it too far. He'd made good progress on the plans and would email the ideas to his usual architect mate to get his perspective.

For now, he needed sleep. Already showered and teeth cleaned after dinner, it was a no-brainer to switch the laptop off and fall onto his swag. His 'more comfortable than her bed' swag. Smiling at Eva's description was the last thing he did before sleep took over and before he had a chance to worry about what nightmares that night would procure.

Jack groaned and opened an eye. In boxers only, he'd long kicked off the swag outer, comfortable with no covers on the sultry summer night. Sprawled on his stomach with his legs splayed in both directions, a spasm ripped through him. He rolled onto his back as his heart sped up.

"Holy shoot," he whispered into the surrounding quiet. He'd slept through the night. No panic attacks, no nightmares, just blessed sleep, like he needed to catch up on a lifetime of it. He sat up and looked around. Ploughing a hand through his hair, his gaze snagged on the bloody wardrobe. With a tank full of sleep under his belt, he waited for the usual panic. He tensed just in case everything changed in an instant.

When nothing happened, he questioned whether he was still sleeping and pinched his arm. *Nope. I'm awake.* Allowing his breathing to return to normal, he rubbed his hand over his face and chuckled at the same time. How long had he slept for? He stumbled up and went searching for his phone.

His stomach grumbled while he tapped the front of his phone. It was one pm—nine hours of sleep.

He swallowed a chuckle and let the phone slip onto the kitchen bench. This was the first sign that maybe he could get past this hurdle. It hadn't seemed possible until then, but it gave him some hope he might be able to keep the promise he made to his mother.

She had tried so hard for him, and the guilt that he had never fulfilled it hadn't gone anywhere. Maybe if he didn't live here full-time, it could be his home away from home.

This revelation was huge, and for the first time in a long time, he wanted to share it with someone. Eva's face was the first to pop up. He double-checked his phone. She would be at the roo park. He scrubbed a hand over his face and made for the shower. He needed to get changed and have some breakfast, fast. This compulsion wouldn't go away, and he'd get there faster if he hiked through the forest. Her trail of bright pink flagging tape would lead him there in a flash.

Yes! Eva would understand the magnitude of what had just happened. He wiped away a light sheen of sweat already building upon his brow. The humidity hovered thickly inside the house. He hadn't taken a glimpse outside yet, but memories of his childhood and other storms invaded his thoughts as he splashed water over his face.

One was undoubtedly brewing.

CHAPTER 19

Eva left the chattering group of seniors cutting up fruit under the covered enclosure and anxiously looked at the sky. She had two choices: duck inside Dr Karen's home and sit in the toilet for the storm's duration, or before it hit, make an excuse and dash home. This was her preferred option. She could cower in her usual spot between the bed and wardrobe where nothing had touched her in the past. Then she wouldn't have to hide the paralysing fear that her thirtieth birthday was the next day.

She swallowed the lump blocking her throat, aware that Harold had been trying to corner her since his arrival an hour ago. Today of all days, she didn't want to be sidetracked, stopping her from getting away if she needed to. Another glance up; the angry, black clouds were quickly building, rolling and blooming. She had half an hour up her sleeve at most.

Harold had detached himself from the group and was making his way to where she would feed the babies. She sighed and beckoned him over. With Dr Karen preparing the milk, she could spend a few minutes chatting with him.

His stiff, elderly gait made him look older than he was. His hair was a shock of grey and his face heavily lined. He hadn't been kind to his body. His broken past and alcohol abuse didn't excuse his treatment of his son and wife. Instead, it saddened Eva how a vicious cycle could continue over more than one generation.

"Take a seat, Harold. How are you today?"

Harold grimaced as he held a steadying hand on the seat's frame and sat down. "I hoped you might have come to visit me sooner."

Eva winced. She always made time for Harold and the other seniors, often bringing a tree kangaroo to the aged-care facility and sharing the joy of learning about these wonderful animals. It wasn't her nature to constantly use work as an excuse, but it was the truth for some weeks. Add Jack to the equation and Harold never got a look in.

"He's good, Harold," she offered first. "He's taken good care of himself."

The relief was palpable in his expression until anxiety skittered across it. "Has he asked about me?"

Eva shook her head. When Dr Karen appeared with the first bottle, she went to get Tommy before settling next to Harold to feed the joey.

"I don't blame him, Evie. I just wish I'd had the balls to tell his mother why I was such a brute and given her the chance to leave and live her own life."

Harold looked crestfallen, and Eva swallowed back the wad of emotion stuck in her throat. He didn't drink these days, but his bloodshot eyes never recovered from the years of abuse. Red lines crisscrossed the whites and now they filled with moisture. His rheumy hand removed a handkerchief from his pocket and dabbed it at his eyes. She knew what he was thinking. That it was too late for any attempt at reconciliation. It was probably true.

She'd become his Evie on the day she somehow managed to break his sullen silence. Their relationship, similar to a father and daughter, blossomed ever since. Now with Jack in the equation and both sides of the story aired, it was hard for her to choose a side. Trauma filled both Jack and Harold's childhoods. Harold's was the unthinkable kind that had left her gasping when she heard his story.

With her time running out, there'd be little chance she could help Harold and Jack come to an understanding about it. That they both needed help to heal was obvious but way out of her sphere of experience. She had no idea how to share her knowledge of what she knew about Harold with Jack, and it tore at her heart. Would it be enough to sour everything between them?

The slurp of an empty bottle distracted Eva from her thoughts. "I'll go get the next roo, and then tell you some things he's told me about himself." It was the least she could do to bring a smidgen of happiness into Harold's tortured existence.

As she rose, Harold smiled his gratitude at this small offering. The ache in Eva's chest expanded to fill her entire body. These days Harold appeared grateful for so little—enough to get him through whatever remaining years he had left. She understood this better than most and would beg Jack's forgiveness when he learnt about her friendship with his father.

She gave Tommy a tender cuddle before putting him back in his enclosure. The yard dipped into darkness when a shadow crossed overhead. She licked dry lips, and her heart felt like it would thump out of her chest.

Eva took off her cotton hat and used it to wipe the beads

of sweat off her face. Rivulets ran a course down her back, and the oppressive humidity weighed on her conscience. She drew in deep and agonised breaths. She owed it to Harold for ignoring him the past few weeks, but she'd do anything to save her own skin if it meant spending one more day with Jack.

She stood transfixed, wavering with her decision. Shoving her hat back on, she dashed back to Harold and noticed he was getting up out of the chair. A small whirlwind picked up loose leaves and whipped her ponytail across her face. The sudden cooling temperature increased the excited chatter of the seniors and other volunteers. They downed tools and watched the clouds roll and darken. It was these moments before a storm, when the coming relief from the suffocating heat was too overwhelming, that stirred up excitement. For Eva, it had the opposite effect. It left her with paralysing fear.

With a close eye on the brewing storm, she offered her arm for Harold to hold and walked him back to the others. "I have to leave, Harold. My windows are open, and I need to go home and close them. I'll be back after the storm." This wasn't a complete lie, but she'd live with it. A lean-to protected the seniors from getting wet when the torrent dropped; Dr Karen could care for them.

Harold must've been grateful to hear she was coming back because he beamed a smile that caused her breath to hitch. It reminded her so much of Jack.

She gasped when the real Jack appeared at her side, the top half of his shirt drenched in sweat, an unreadable expression on his face. Was it disgust? Eva tightened her hold on Harold when she swayed with dizziness, confused by Jack's sudden appearance. Had he witnessed Harold's smile and guessed they were friends? Or was it a double of Harold she saw, only in her mind a younger version? She darted a glance between them. Surely the coming storm wasn't causing her to see things?

Jack's cutting words cleared her head in an instant. "You knew him all along?" His viciousness stung, a storm of his own brewing behind eyes that changed into swirling black clouds.

Harold managed the last few steps on his own, releasing Eva's arm. She turned and faced Jack, reaching for him, but he shoved her hand away. "Jack, please—"

"You've been lying to me all this time?" His chest heaved like he'd run a marathon.

"Son, *please*, let her explain," Harold said, trying to stand.

Jack backed off and pointed at Harold's chest. "Keep away from me, you bastard." Sweat dripped off his brow as the intensifying wind ruffled his hair. His eyes flared with rage.

A sense of loss enveloped Eva. This was too soon. "Let me explain, Jack," she yelled as the wind whipped her hat off her head and sent it twirling into the air before landing in the yard. As Jack turned and sprinted towards the track leading back to the forest, her words were lost or ignored.

The storm that erupted overhead brought the blackness that had been inching closer to her thirtieth birthday. It had been her greatest fear all her life, and she'd been right to believe so. Except, she wanted one last chance at life.

Throwing caution to the wind, she took off after Jack, ignoring common sense dictating she got to the safety of her car. Her heart was ruling, and she may as well die like the curse expected her to if it meant losing Jack.

Anger drove Jack's fast pace. He slashed his arms at branches as he glimpsed the occasional piece of bright pink flagging tape. Thunder was rolling above the canopy, and the heavens opened up, but the forest protected him from the worst. He thought he heard his name called from behind but didn't stop to check. If it was Eva, he couldn't face her, not now he suspected she knew about him all along. What about Mick? Was he in on it too? Had Jack really fallen for the viral Kenny story? *Bloody hell!* His curse was lost in the furore of mother nature as lightning struck close by and thunder rattled the surrounding earth.

The short distance from the edge of the forest to the back of the house was enough to drench him thoroughly. He slipped getting up the three steps to the verandah and collapsed when his legs buckled. Taking in lungs full of air, his head fell back as he attempted to get his breathing back to normal.

Seconds later, he sat bolt upright when he *did* hear his name. It was a piercing sound.

"Jack!"

Terror had transformed Eva's expression into someone unrecognisable, and despite the heavy rain, tears streamed down her face. She stumbled up the stairs and rushed past him into the house. Jack jumped to his feet and followed, confusion marring his thoughts when he lost sight of her.

"Eva!" The downpour dulled every sound, including his shout. "Eva!" he tried again. His chest constricted tenfold when her wet footprints led to the wardrobe.

Momentarily, he couldn't move. Flashbacks of his childhood time spent in that confined space as punishment flashed before his eyes, almost in time with the lightning. He sucked in a breath and slowly walked towards it. Now that he knew where she was, her uncontrollable sobs were distinct.

Each one wracked against his chest the closer he got. The thunder boomed in his ears for a different reason now.

He knelt and tried to open the door with shaking hands. It wouldn't budge at first, so he tried again. "Eva," he begged, "let go of the door." There was a little latch she was holding onto. He remembered it well.

"Eva, open up," he pleaded.

"Go away!"

Jack fell onto his backside and rocked back and forth. Two would never fit inside, not that he had any intention of ever doing so. But something had set her off. He'd never seen an expression so stricken with terror before.

"Eva," he tried again, but softer this time, "let me hold your hand."

He waited with bated breath, sitting frozen to the spot. Too scared to leave, too terrified to push further. With the storm at its peak, lightning lit the room and thunder exploded. The rain continued to pummel the roof and windows.

His eyes remained rooted to the edge of the door until a thin sliver of its edge appeared. When her wet hand snaked out, he grasped it and squeezed it once. She squeezed back, but neither spoke.

It was enough that they were connected. The skin-on-skin contact was holding everything in place. He never imagined he'd look at the wardrobe as anything but a place of terror and darkness while Eva sat inside the damn thing, reaping some comfort from its small, dank interior. He almost smiled at the irony of it but didn't. One day he might, but not until he understood what had upset Eva.

As the time passed, the darkness of the storm slowly vanished, and the brilliant afternoon made its return. Just as the clearing clouds signalled the worst was over, Eva's sobs subsided. Jack continued to sit, mesmerised by her hand. His thumb gently stroked her tanned and healthy skin, his thoughts returning to the shock of seeing his father again. Anger tried to burst its way up his throat, so he concentrated on Eva's hand and let its softness tamper it down.

There had to be a reason Eva kept it a secret from him. So, he waited patiently, the same way he had for the many hours locked in this wardrobe.

Relaxing slightly, he leant back against it. He wasn't going anywhere. In the same square metre space where he dreamt of being a pilot, Jack knew with certainty that his life revolved around Eva. How, he wasn't so certain, and the why, well, that was as clear as mud. This caused him to chuckle, and Eva's hand jerked in his.

"Jack," she whispered with a sniffle, "are you okay?"

Jack smiled and squeezed her hand. "I will be once you start talking again."

"Sorry about forcing you near this thing."

"I only wish I could fit in with you."

"You what? Huh?"

"That's what I was coming to tell you this afternoon. I slept through the night without any nightmares. I think I can do this, Eva."

The door nudged against his thigh.

"Are you going to let some air in for me?" she asked in a raspy voice.

Laughter burst from his throat as he shuffled back, allowing the small door to swing open.

"It's very musty in here, and since I can't leave here until tomorrow, I'll—"

"What?" Jack cut in, confused. He peered inside and latched onto her blotchy face. "Why?"

"Because my thirtieth birthday is tomorrow, and I'm supposed to die by then."

"You're what!" Jack yelped, the sound echoing around the empty room. His heart pumped furiously. He dropped her hand and rose on unsteady legs, pacing the room. How did someone plan a death? Was Eva contemplating suicide? No fucking way! He wasn't going to lose a second person this way, and so help him, if his father was responsible in some way, he'd lose it. And then *anything* could happen.

He stopped pacing in front of the wardrobe and planted his hands on his hips. "Is my father getting to you?"

"No! Oh, God no, Jack, what are you talking about?" Eva slid out of the wardrobe and stood with a supporting hand on the door, her wet clothes plastered to her body.

"Stay away from him. He's a monster. You know nothing about him."

Eva took a tentative step toward him. "Jack, he's not anymore. He's really not."

Jack wailed pitifully. Enough that a shard of pain pierced his chest. "Oh my God. You believe that?" He ploughed a hand roughly through his wet hair and turned away from her innocent gesture when her hand reached for his.

"Jack, listen to me. There's stuff you don't know."

Jack was close enough to the wardrobe to kick the small door, getting no satisfaction from the jarring noise when it connected.

"No, you listen to me," Jack spat. "You became friends with my father, and you never told me? That's going down really well, just so you know. Then he tells you some hyped-up story about how fabulous he is, but he doesn't tell you the truth."

Jack blinked furiously. No way was he going to shed a single tear in front of Eva. But the memories came crashing down around him, and he used both hands to cover his head, as though something could fall from the sky and kill him on the spot.

"Jack, let me tell you *his* story," Eva persisted.

"His story!" he yelled back. "What did it entail, *Eva*? Did he mention how he drank every day? Did he tell you how a day rarely went by without him physically abusing my mother? Did he add how many times he kept me locked in that damn wardrobe you just came out of? Did he enlighten you about how he pushed my mother so far that she took her own life?"

Eva remained still, squaring her shoulders, taking the questions he was hurtling at her.

Breathing had become difficult. Tears hovered so bloody dangerously close that he lifted his wet tee-shirt and used it to press against his face.

"Jack," Eva whispered, her words barely audible, "he *did* tell me all this. He also told me his own father and uncle sexually abused him for many years. A lot of those times, they abused him together."

His breath hitched in his throat. If he didn't move another inch, would he stop breathing? His hand dropped by his side at Eva's bombshell. It was certainly a moment when death sounded like the better alternative.

His gaze levelled with Eva's, and there it was again. The pitying looks he'd seen before. A spasm shook his shoulders and dislodged his tongue. "And you've known him for how long?"

"I met him about five years ago when I started coming here. Your mother's death was *the* wake-up call, and he told me he stopped drinking the day she was buried. For you, for her, it was too late. I get that. I think he finally got it too. I began taking him to my family of babies and the roo park to help him reconnect with the community. He never left home except for the basics of food and paying some bills." Eva's gaze was intense, watching him closely until she released a big sigh. "I'll admit my intentions were to get on his good side so that I could protect my family living on his property. Actually, the volunteers tasked me with the job of befriending him. God knows why I persisted. He was a sullen, unhappy man, but somehow, I just kept talking."

Despite the turmoil raging through his head, Jack smiled wryly. He dropped to the swag and wrapped his arms around his knees. He understood the power of Eva's talking.

"One day, while we sat in my usual spot in the forest, he opened up. Told me how he ran away from home at fourteen. Talked about his father and uncle. How he lived in the bush, on the streets, somehow always finding a meal. He never went back, not even for his mother. His hate transcended all boundaries, coating his heart, coating his soul. Eventually, he picked up some part-time work and began earning money. He put some aside, and it was enough to impress your mother when he found full-time work with the council here. The same one your grandfather was mayor of."

Jack loosened his hold on his knees and raked both hands through his hair. His fingers clenched around the wet clumps.

"I'm sorry, Jack. I know I should've told you sooner, but I didn't know how to. After telling me the truth, all your father could talk about was how his greatest fear had been he would hurt you. There was so much anger in him that he was protecting you by locking you away."

"Bullshit!" Jack spat, slapping his hand on the swag, but it didn't stop Eva from spilling out more of his father's regrets. Her talking went on and on and he pressed his hands against his ears, but they couldn't shut out her words. What did he care if she knew his favourite treat as a kid was his mother's homemade choc-chip biscuits? His father *remembered* that?

"He's had lots of counselling since, but talking about it still hurts. He's told me how beautiful your mother was and how he slowly killed her as if his own hands had done it. But what he talks about the most is you. A son he wishes he could connect with again. A son he'd do anything to say 'I'm sorry' to. He'll carry those regrets to his grave."

"Stop it!" Jack jumped up and stormed outside.

"Jack, wait!" Eva shouted through the vibrating noise of the door slamming behind him.

He didn't want to wait. But this was Eva, and she didn't know how to back off. The door screeched open, and her booted footsteps stomped down the three steps towards the backyard. With a mind of their own, his legs took him to the forest, to the one place where he might make sense of this.

Eva followed. She didn't need to speak for him to feel her presence. How was he supposed to sort the mess out in his head if she didn't give him some space? "Go away, Eva," he growled back over his shoulder.

"No. Way. Jack."

"You'll scare your babies."

"I don't care," came her response.

At the family of trees, water dripped off the leaves, landing on his face with little bursts of ice on his hot and flushed skin. The overpowering forest fragrance was filled with too much moisture. It overloaded his senses so that he could only take little breaths.

Before he plonked himself on the damp forest undergrowth at their favourite tree, he rounded on her and barked, "Why are you considering suicide? Why tell me something like that after everything we've been through? Is this my father's sick mind getting to you? Are you terminally ill?"

"What?" Eva shrieked, causing the roos to scurry above them. "What are you talking about?"

"Your own words, Eva. You're supposed to die by your birthday. How does anyone know when their last day is unless they're planning it?"

The tears tumbled down her cheeks, and her shoulders sagged. "Oh, Jack, why would I contemplate something like that? I'm so desperate to live another day."

He frowned. "What's stopping you?"

"The curse."

"The what?"

"You heard me damn it," she shouted, lifting *her* wet shirt to wipe at her face. "Do you think I have any choice?"

"Eva"—Jack wilted at the agony on her face and went to her—"please tell me what's going on." He wound his arms around her shuddering shoulders, hoping to calm the same uncontrollable sobbing he first witnessed when she ran out of the storm and into the wardrobe.

With no chance of her crying stopping, he lifted and cradled her in his arms and sat in their spot. All the while, he kissed her temple and eyes with feather kisses, adding soothing words to calm her. He would have to deal with his all-consuming anger about her friendship with his father another day. It would tear at him if he didn't expose her reasons for lying, but he understood the importance of sorting through this matter first.

When she stemmed her flow of grief, she pulled back and swiped her arm over her face before snuggling closer. She tried to hide her puffy and blotchy face, but Jack didn't care. To him, she was beautiful, and for a split second, he stiffened, recalling Eva's words about how his father thought his mother was beautiful, too. This was enough to change his mind and ask her something else first. "Did you know Mick was a good mate of mine?"

She looked up with a startled gaze and nodded. Through her sniffles, she said, "I'm sorry, Jack, I really am. He had no idea you were back. He hadn't connected the viral Kenny video with you until I told him. I asked him to check on you after your first night at the house alone. I knew you wouldn't have an easy time, but I didn't feel it was my place to do so."

Angry swirls twisted inside his stomach. Not directed at Mick. He was a good mate and understood his turmoils better than most. Not directed at Eva. She'd come onto the scene long after his father had done all the damage. It wasn't her fault that her instinct was to care about others, even if she'd chosen to help the wrong person. No, as usual, his anger was directed at his father. He wanted to give it a rest, but his head wouldn't let him. "I never want anything to do with my father again. You realise this, don't you?"

"I know," she whispered, "that's why I couldn't bring myself to tell you the truth. It would send you packing and I wasn't prepared to let that happen. The longer I held off, the harder it got. I'm so sorry, Jack. I don't deserve you, but with my time running out, I got so damn selfish; I had no intention of ruining what we had. Bringing your father into the conversation would have done it."

Jack sighed and scrubbed his free hand over his face.

"Jack?"

He relaxed a smidgen at the sound of his name. Processing his father's story was for another day. He angled his face and pushed her gently away. "Will you explain what's going on?"

Like a spring needing to jolt back into place, she resisted

his hold and placed her cheek back against his warmth. "Yeah, I suppose I better."

Jack rested his chin on top of her head and grimaced. He had to push aside the anger and make an effort. He'd lost his mother way too early and didn't want a bar of his father, but he wasn't losing Eva. Ever.

CHAPTER 20

Where did Eva start? She kept her hands wound around Jack's neck after he insisted on carrying her back to the house. With her face nestled in the nook between his neck and shoulder, she inhaled his scent, a combination of sweat, moisture, male and that ever-present touch of pine. She let it fill her head, her tense shoulders sagging at the relief it brought. The more relaxed she could stay, the easier it would be to explain things.

Once inside the house, Jack slid the swag up against the wardrobe and passed her the spare pillow. She was determined to spend the remaining hours until her birthday in the enclosed space. Perplexed as he looked, Jack didn't argue.

"Make yourself comfortable," he said before walking out of the bare-walled living room and down the short hallway.

On his return, he was stripped of his wet clothes and wore boxers only. "Here"—he handed her a white shirt—"put this on. If you're not coming out, you need to get out of those wet clothes."

She didn't argue and curled up tight enough to remove her sodden clothes in the confined space. When she put on his oversized cotton shirt, it wasn't enough to stop the shivering that had set in. It could've been from the drenching, but Eva suspected it was a few things rolled into one.

"Bloody hell, Eva, I can't warm you from out here." Jack raced away again. He returned with a worn pair of track pants and a jumper. "Get into these, quick."

With her shaking worsening, she pulled on his warm offerings and lay down. Filling her lungs with the essence of Jack that clung to his clothing, she curled her knees up to her chest, hoping to draw in as much warmth as possible.

Exhaustion gripped her limbs as she relaxed for the first time since the storm's onset. She doubted she could move from this spot even if she wanted to. Maybe this was how it was all going to end, but she was with Jack, and for now, she didn't care.

When her eyes fluttered closed, she sensed Jack had gone somewhere again. He was muttering something, and then lifting her wet hair and putting a towel beneath it. Eva smiled in her drowsy state. Most of her short length was inside the wardrobe, but her head sat at the door that Jack wrenched back as far as the hinges would allow. She should have been embarrassed by all this, but she wasn't. It made perfect sense to cower away in this spot for the remaining hours until she turned thirty.

Jack lay on his swag and stroked her wet hair away from her face, and she could feel the warmth of his face beside hers. His breath on her skin helped bring life back to her frozen form, and nothing in the world could halt the tears as they re-emerged and trickled down her cheeks.

"Hey, it's going to be okay." Jack continued to stroke her hair and kissed her forehead. "I'm not going anywhere."

Eva managed a nod. All the fears she'd kept locked away ever since she was old enough to understand things were finally exposed. If that meant crying and shaking uncontrollably, what choice did she have?

She willed sleep to come, but it was a futile wish. And anyway, she wanted to live every second of her remaining time before midnight struck to remind her of how old she was.

Jack started at the sound of vehicles arriving, and his hand stopped its soothing touch. "Don't move. I'll see who it is."

Eva had the sudden urge to grab hold of his hand and prevent him from leaving her side, but Jack was up and walking towards the front door before her lethargic muscles could move an inch. Instead, her tears intensified as she attempted to muffle their sound on the pillow.

When Jack returned, she heard the rattle of keys and recognised the sound of a little charm she carried on her keyring. Before Jack shut the front door, a second vehicle departed.

"That was Dr Karen and her husband. They brought your ute over and wanted to check we were both okay."

Eva lifted her face when Jack lay down again, and she tried to stem her tears.

Jack pierced her gaze with a determined look. "I told her I'm taking care of you."

Eva nodded and rested her eyes closed again. Dr Karen knew nothing of her fears. Warmth finally found its way to most of her extremities, and she rubbed her fingers against her palms to ease their stiffness. How on earth was she going to start this conversation?

She jolted when an idea came to her. "Jack"—she cleared her throat when his name came out croaky—"could you please go to my ute and get my backpack. It's on the front seat. There's something I keep that might help make sense of what I'm going to say."

Jack was up instantly, collecting her keys off the floor near the door where he left them. On his return, he sat cross-legged and placed the backpack down.

Looking at her seriously, he said, "Okay, Eva, time to talk."

Despite fear swirling around her head and her blubbery state, she managed a crooked smile. She crawled out of the wardrobe, leaving her feet inside it. Crazy, she knew, but she couldn't help it. Small, dark places had always protected her in the past.

She unzipped the small front pocket on the backpack where she kept her wallet. What she searched for was only small, but she'd laminated it, and it fit neatly in a zipped pocket. Occasionally, she pulled it out and looked at it when the need arose.

Eva swallowed nervously and looked up to find Jack's gaze latched onto her face. He wore his serious and brooding look, the one she'd come to love. "Jack, I hope what I'm about to tell you doesn't make me sound crazy."

A hint of a smile touched the edges of his mouth as his hand squeezed her shoulder. "You were crazy from the first moment I met you, and it's stayed with me ever since. There you were, dead gorgeous, all woman, kitted up, ready to save a blind tree kangaroo. And you drive a ute. Doesn't come any sexier or crazier."

"Aww … Jack." She swiped unsteadily at her tear-streaked cheeks.

"Shhh, don't cry, please."

He opened his arms, and she hesitated, looking at the open wardrobe door before shuffling closer, welcoming his embrace. When they tightened around her, a sense of peace settled over her. If she went out feeling this way, she'd be satisfied. Except, she wanted to outwit this damn curse.

She picked up her wallet from where it'd slipped to the floor. Tucked inside at the very back, she drew out a small, laminated newspaper article and passed it to Jack. "Read this."

"Can I read it out aloud?"

Eva nodded, her fingers twisting in knots, hoping her reasons for her fear after all these years sounded logical.

"Three-year-old Eva Stamford was found alive, tucked between the protective care of three rare Lumholtz tree kangaroos on the forest floor, only metres from where her deceased mother was found, killed instantly by what appears to be a severe lightning strike."

Jack gasped. There was a pained look in his eyes. She knew the photo so well. It was a little blurry but clearly showed a small child's arm tucked in between bundles of fur. Considering how sensitive the tree kangaroo was to intrusive noise, Eva always considered the lucky snap a miracle. The tree kangaroos would've bounded away within seconds, leaving her in the care of the rescue team.

"They found her fast asleep and warm, despite the search team taking until the morning to locate her."

"So, that's where your fierce love of the tree kangaroo comes from," Jack said, still studying the photo.

There wasn't much more of the article to read, but he'd stated the obvious. "I knew one day I'd come back and devote my time to them. I owed them so much; it was the least I could do."

"Except this doesn't explain the curse bit."

"No," and her eyes filled again.

"Hey"—Jack reached for her—"lie down and let me hold you. Damn, this is really upsetting you."

Eva nodded and sniffled at the same time. She used the shirt to dab at her eyes and inhaled a shaky breath. "My mum was a day shy of her thirtieth birthday. Dad told me she loved going for forest walks. It wasn't unusual that she'd taken me. She'd fed my younger sister and left her sleeping in the pram with Dad while he did some repairs on the car. The storm hadn't brewed yet, so Dad said he wasn't too worried. He knew Mum wouldn't be too long, but then the storm came from nowhere and fast. It was only a small destructive cell, but it left severe damage to the forest and the path it struck."

A shiver shook her torso at the memory of how quickly that day's storm had brewed, and Jack tightened his hold.

"You okay?"

Eva nodded, knowing she had to go on. "The storm cut the power, and when Mum hadn't turned up soon after, Dad panicked. It also damaged the phone connection. He'd never felt so helpless and, of course, he had a one-year-old baby with him. By the time he alerted the rescue authorities and they started the search, it was already night. They continued looking during the night, but they didn't find us until the morning."

Jack kissed her forehead tenderly. "I'm sorry, that's horribly tragic, but"—he softly kneaded her back—"it doesn't explain the curse."

Eva grimaced and buried her face against Jack's neck.

Jack took hold of her shoulders and gently pried her back. "Tell me, Eva."

Eva chewed her bottom lip, unsure how this would sound. "My grandmother on Mum's side died a day before her thirtieth birthday. If you can believe it, she was struck by lightning too. She was the eldest daughter in her family, and so was Mum."

Jack gasped, and his brows knitted. "Really?"

Eva nodded. "I must've been about eight years old when I overheard some relatives talking about it and making fun of it like it was some joke. My little heart thumped for days when I realised I was the eldest girl in my family."

"Bloody hell," Jack swore, "and I bet you've been holding onto that little gem ever since," he added sarcastically.

Eva could only pinch her lips and nod as her shabby attempt to stop the tears failed.

Jack released her and flopped onto his back. He rolled to his side and watched her intently. "So, you just have to get to midnight safely and the curse is no longer valid. Right? Is it as simple as that?"

Eva shrugged, not sure about anything.

"Your grandmother and mother both died just before their thirtieth?"

She nodded, drawing up the bottom of her shirt again to mop her face.

"Right. So, if you don't move from this spot and I get you to midnight safely, you're free of it."

The absurdity of what he was saying and wanting to do, brought about an agonising chuckle that doubled the torrent of tears.

"Hey," he comforted, "I'll make us some toasted sandwiches and bring out a pack of cards. Look, we're down to single digits when it comes to the number of hours we have left."

"You don't think I'm crazy?" she managed to say between gulps of air and a stuffy nose.

The late afternoon sun dazzled into the musty old house and captured Jack in one of its brilliant rays. The tender look he gave her stilled her crying and caused her breath to hitch. "No more than I am, but if I ever learn who made those stupid remarks when you were a kid, I'll smite them myself."

Eva laughed and sobbed some more. Her fear and

constant anxiety had strangled her for most of her life. She'd never spoken a word about it to anyone until now. Jack's words were some sort of release. Well, not completely until midnight struck, but a start.

Jack tilted his head and eyed her speculatively. "You know what's going to happen at midnight, don't you?"

Eva sat up, keeping one foot in the wardrobe, and looked down at Jack. For once in her life, she was mute. She'd never considered life after that moment.

He reached across and squeezed her hand before shuffling closer to kiss the inside of her wrist. It sent a tingle up her arm, causing a delightful shiver across her chest.

With her hand limp in his, he said, "I'm going to ask you whether you'd be interested in giving us a go."

"Us?"

He nodded, a vulnerable look crossing his face. Like she'd ever consider refusing such an offer. If she got past the curse.

After a beat, she found her tongue. "Yes," she uttered on a sigh, "the way you say 'us' sounds perfect."

The smile that made its way across Jack's face was huge, and there was not a skerrick of broodiness to be seen.

"Get me safely to midnight," Eva begged, "please."

Jack sat up and lifted her onto his lap.

"My foot, Jack. It has to stay in the wardrobe."

Her silly request didn't faze him at all. He manoeuvred her so that her foot remained inside, but the rest of her, it seemed, belonged to him. When his mouth found hers, she admitted she had no idea whether her foot remained inside the wardrobe.

Their kiss went on for ages. Even the sun decided it was tired of their antics and called it a night. When the first shadow fell across where they sat, Jack's stomach grumbled.

She pulled back a fraction and gulped much-needed air. "You need food."

"I've found it," Jack uttered, commanding possession of her mouth again.

A small burst of laughter escaped, causing Jack to stop. He quizzed her with a quirked brow.

"I'll be too nervous to eat, but you better have that toasted sandwich you bragged about."

Jack smiled, sweet and sexy all in one, and touched her eyes with wispy, featherlike kisses. "Still not overly impressed with my cooking skills, are you?"

"I'll teach you," Eva assured him, closing her eyes and enjoying the places his mouth touched.

"Changing me already, are you?"

"Yup," was her smiling reply, as they lay down again and forgot about food for a little while longer.

EPILOGUE

"They're here," Jack shouted back into the house.

Eva wiped the bead of sweat off her brow and went to wash her hands in the partly demolished bathroom.

She took every opportunity to invite Mick and Jillian over. Their two rascal boys loved nothing more than visiting her babies in the forest, and Eva took them as often as they could come. She was certain eight-month-old Natalie's first word was 'roo'.

On her way outside, she dodged ladders and construction paraphernalia the building team were using for the renovations. They knew the noise was to be kept to a minimum and no one was to disturb the forest. Stepping over piles of rubble and walking around bundles of timber, she would have to be careful the boys didn't run riot inside.

By the end of the makeover, Eva was sure Jack would never recognise the interior of his old childhood home. For that, she was glad. The only trademark feature to remain was the tulip-featured balcony his maternal grandfather had handcrafted himself. She ran her finger lovingly over one of its edges before skipping down the three steps.

The more she learnt about Jack's grandfather, the more impressed she was. Keeping the balcony intact was a fitting tribute to a fine man.

"Hello, everyone." Without hesitating, she went for Natalie, who had her arms out, ready to be taken. Eva hugged her close and inhaled the baby smells she hoped one day would come her way.

"Who's ready to see my tree kangaroos?" Eva asked Johnny and Trevor.

"Me, me, me," they chorused.

"Have we all got shoes on?" As she inspected their feet, Eva looked across as Mick helped their extra passenger. Jack always tensed whenever his father was close, and without him being aware, his broodiness took over. Sometimes it was only momentary, but she sensed Jack's internal struggle to adapt to his father's presence.

Cautiously, Harold had entered their lives, seeking Jack first. Jack fought against his better judgement for many months before letting Harold tell his story. Not until the day Harold declared he loved Jack so much he'd leave him alone, did Jack change his mind.

Jack had taken him to his special spot in the forest, hoping it might work its magic. Under the guidance of a dozen tree kangaroos, Jack spilled out his anger and hurt. Harold, in turn, shared with Jack the torture and anguish of his childhood. It was early days, but Eva hoped that one day they might find themselves on the same path. It wasn't something she expected would happen overnight, but more likely over many years. If at all.

"What about a hat?" Eva asked the boys.

They giggled. "You always ask us that. We don't need a hat, Aunty Eva."

Eva smiled. "Okay, you win. I'll get some mats out of the house to sit on."

Jack was by her side in an instant. "Here, let me, you always hog her."

"But I just got her."

They fought like cats and dogs over who would hold Natalie the most. Jack always won because Eva loved the sight of Jack with a child in his arms. It suited him, and he looked so at home it made her yearn to be a mother one day.

"And now it's my turn," he said while his mouth sought hers for a quick and urgent kiss.

"Yuck," Johnny declared, running circles on the green lawn, "Jack kissed Aunty Eva."

Little Trevor ran on his chubby legs and repeated, "Yuck, yuck, yuck."

The kids did it every time. They broke the tension and had the adults laughing. Harold and Jack included.

Eva gave up Natalie to Jack's waiting arms, then dashed up the steps for the yoga mats she kept in a tub inside the front door.

She stopped and held her breath every time she spotted the old wardrobe in the living room. It was the one thing she fought with Jack to keep. It'd taken him a while to come around, but she couldn't bear to see the old thing thrown out. Harold had told her once he initially planned on burning it, leaving no reminders for Jack. A prolonged illness had kept Harold from getting it done before Jack returned.

Gone was the old, stained timber look. Eva asked a dear friend to paint a delightful mural of rainbows and sunshine, rainforest and tree kangaroos, and a girl and a boy with a surprising resemblance to herself and Jack. She was more than pleased with the results. Now that Jack had pried the doors off, she'd added some shelves and placed photos and other knick-knacks on them.

On the night of her thirtieth birthday, the storms hadn't ended with that first one. At about eleven pm that night, another burst of lightning had crackled overhead, and she had cowered inside the wardrobe one last time, certain it'd come back to finally claim her.

After so many years of anxiety-driven fear, in her mind and her mind alone, the wardrobe had saved her life. She didn't want to be parted from it. When midnight had finally come and gone, she'd fallen into an exhausted sleep and awoken to a startling beautiful morning. She'd beaten the curse.

They hadn't asked too many questions about the future, except for taking it one day at a time. Jack had taken another year of leave as they slowly transformed the house. They also continued doing everything to save the tree kangaroo, which Jack helped with occasional monetary donations, and enjoyed the life she was certain she'd never get.

She darted one more look at the wardrobe before dashing out the door with the mats tucked under her arm.

Jack waited at the bottom of the steps with Natalie fast asleep in his arms. "Not eyeing off that wardrobe again, were you? I already promised you the damn thing could stay."

"Was there ever a possibility of it going?" Her heart danced inside her chest. He knew her so well, and she reached up to give him a lingering kiss over the sleeping toddler. "I love you, Jack. Thank you for letting us keep it."

Jack groaned. "Why now?" he whispered. "With visitors here and no chance of touching you for hours."

The boys stopped their earlier chanting and began circling their legs, their grubby hands grabbing at the hem of her shorts.

"Johnny, Trevor, you'll wake Natalie," Jillian reprimanded the boys, but with little effect.

Eva stepped back and smiled. "Make it worth my while when you do."

"I'm dying here, Eva, just so you know," he hissed close to her ear.

"Hey, if I can survive past my thirtieth, you'll survive this." She winked.

Jack's shoulders sagged, and Natalie snuffled in her sleep. "Lucky I love you enough," he proclaimed, reaching for another quick peck before turning back to Mick and Harold. "You ready for the walk, Dad?"

Eva's chest burst to exploding. It was the first time Jack had called Harold, Dad. It was a big moment and not one to be taken lightly. Jack probably hadn't realised it himself. She'd remind him of this momentous occasion later, when they were alone again and when they often spoke of things that still hurt. But only after he took her to that special place, high above the earth and into the startling blue of the sky.

The same place he promised to take her in his beloved aircraft.

AUTHOR'S NOTE

The Atherton Tablelands is very fortunate to have a real Dr Karen who has devoted her life to the well-being and care of the Lumholtz tree kangaroo. This variety is unique to this area, but their habitat's gradual disappearance has placed them in the near-threatened category. They do suffer from blindness, and Dr Karen and her band of volunteers will continue to find the means and resources to research why. If you'd like further information, here is a link to the tree roo rescue website page: **https://www.treeroorescue.org.au/**

ALSO BY FRANCES DALL'ALBA

If you haven't read my books in the **Australian at Heart Series**, learn more here.

Little Blue Box, Australian at Heart Book 1 is Ella's story. When plans go astray, can one little blue box put their lives back on the same path?

There's one thing missing in Ella Harvey's life—her biological father. All she has is a few clues in a little box and a mother not willing to share anything. Add in her impatience and stubbornness and Ella decides to go about finding him herself.

Then there's Zane. He's used to barrelling his way through life without too much stress. He has a great family, a new career path and a beloved Ducati motorcycle.

When tasked with searching for Ella's father, Zane discovers a secret that threatens to unravel their lives.

The attraction between Zane and Ella is flaring up quickly, but all will go up in flames if Zane doesn't tell Ella what he knows.

Ella finds out the hard way that searching for the truth doesn't always go to plan. She'll bundle up Zane's heart, wrap it up tight and hand it back to him. Problem solved and no one gets hurt.

But Zane won't give Ella up. To keep the gorgeous Ella by his side, he had to find her father. To keep the woman he's now fallen in love with, he'll have to save her mother.

Will the unexpected twist that comes their way be enough for the head-strong Ella and Ducati-loving Zane to find their way back onto the same path?

Link to Buy this book

https://francesdallalba.wixsite.com/francesdallalba/littlebluebox

The second book in the series, **The Stone In The Road,** is Patrick's story. You meet him briefly in Little Blue Box. Read how he turns his life around and finds his true self with the help of an Aussie girl.

It's been eighteen months since Kelly Sheppard disappeared into the Australian outback. The guilt and regret she carries still won't leave her.

Newly arrived from Boston, Patrick Van Der Meeliko is working hard to get himself back on track—and succeeding. He can thank the Australian outback for healing him in ways his affluent and empty life in Boston could not. Kelly is his new drug of choice, and he can't resist throwing irksome comments her way to try and get her attention. If only it would work.

With men her last priority right now, Kelly does her best to ignore Patrick despite needing to work together. Kelly doesn't know what's worse—his lame jokes or his driving skills.

After Kelly discovers she's inherited her grandfather's property, she heads north. Patrick lands on her doorstep right when she could use the extra help. Amidst the hard work of untangling vines from the derelict castle, an astonishing history emerges and an unexpected chemistry ignites between them.

Until Kelly's parents turn up unannounced, and suddenly there's no room for Patrick in her life. Despite all the pain she's endured, pushing Patrick away hurts the most.

Patrick gets it, and doesn't stand in her way. He must travel his own road littered with uncertainty and doubt to find his rightful place. Once again, it's the Australian outback that heals him.

Could a chance find of a precious stone draw them back together?

Link to Buy this Book

https://francesdallalba.wixsite.com/francesdallalba/
thestoneintheroad

The Silk Scarf is book 3 in the series. This is Melita's story. A silken scarf entwines itself around two hearts. Sometimes it unravels... An emotional and passionate story of romance set in tropical far north Queensland. You can smell the sugar cane and humidity all at once.

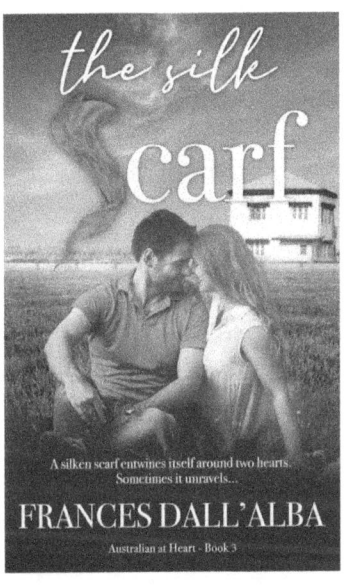

Melita Van Der Meeliko's swimwear is starting to make waves in the industry. Hoping to ride the success, she's determined to open her own boutique/teahouse. A chance find of a derelict building might be the solution—and she wants Luke Harvey to do the renovations. Shaking off her feelings for him is another challenge altogether.

Down-to-earth tradesman Luke Harvey has dreams of his own, determined to be a leader in sustainable green buildings. When Melita offers him the chance to showcase his skills, he's got to make a choice. Turn down the career-making project or risk torturing his heart. His recurring nightmare is one thing, but that wasn't the only reason he ended what they once had.

Deciding to risk it all, Luke takes on the project. Too bad the building has a history, and not a very pleasant one. And Luke doesn't like it when Melita gets caught in the crosshairs.

With Melita's life at risk, Luke recognises the gaping abyss between her ultra-wealthy existence and his barely-there meagre living. Denying it was the reason he pulled back three years earlier won't work anymore. Luke will need to quell his nightmares and let go of the money issue, because Melita wants everything she's worked so hard for and the man she loves.

Will the silk scarf that's entwined itself around their lives stop unravelling, and bring them back together?

Link to Buy this Book

https://francesdallalba.wixsite.com/francesdallalba/thesilkscarf

Book 4 in The Australian At Heart Series is Flynn's story.

Due For Release in 2023.

Eight Seconds, is a stand-alone story inspired by an incredible Australian woman showcased in two Australian Halls of Fame.

Triumph, hardship, true grit...and one crazy dream.

An inspirational story about one woman, with one dream, and one almighty driving passion.

Grace Lucas knows from an early age that climbing onto a bucking animal and holding on is exactly what she wants. When Grace wins her first poddy ride at the age of twelve but is refused the first prize trophy because she's a girl, it stirs a fierce streak that won't rest — not until she's allowed to compete in the sport she loves as an equal and be recognised for it.

Erin Blackwater comes into Grace's life many years after her bull riding days are over, at a time when she has questions and doubts about how her own life is tracking. Employed by a medical research company to record Grace's miracle recovery, Grace teaches Erin the importance of living life to the fullest without fear or regrets. Or life will leave you behind.

Encapsulating the Australian outback landscape of the sixties and seventies, with a storyline weaving in and out of the present day, this story is inspired by one woman, with one dream, and one almighty driving passion. With every adversity in her way, Grace pushes past the barriers and succeeds in a male dominated sport, and creates a new legend.

Link to Buy this Book

https://francesdallalba.wixsite.com/francesdallalba/eightseconds

THANKS FOR READING.

Thank you for reading **Jack & Eva.** Now that you've finished, you'll be a whole lot more familiar with the Lumholtz Tree Kangaroo, which is uniquely found in rainforest fragments of the Atherton Tablelands.

"To entertain the idea that any kangaroo known to us, or approaching its formation, could climb a tree, would be ridiculous..." William Hann 12 October 1872.

They were named after the explorer, Carl Lumholtz, who first found them in 1882. They are **not** nocturnal and you will find them active day and night. Tree kangaroos are also the only kangaroo that can 'walk' or move each foot independently — forward, backwards and bipedal, which is up on its back legs. This assists them when climbing.

Lucky for us, one very special couple, Dr Karen Coombes and her husband Neil McLaughlan, took a special interest in them when they moved from the Northern Territory and made their home on the Atherton Tablelands.

They converted their property to the **Tree Roo Rescue and Conservation Centre**, a non-profit organisation that rescues and rehabilitates orphaned, injured, or displaced tree kangaroos. They work at releasing them back into the wild, or if that is not possible, for life in captivity as breeding animals for education and conservation in zoos.

As Dr Karen will tell us, the Lumholtz Tree Kangaroo is a 'near threatened' species with their biggest threat being loss of habitat, dogs and being hit by cars when moving between forests. Dr Karen and her team will continue to advocate for this adorable animal and continue the research into why there is also an increase in blindness.

So, thank you Dr Karen and Neil, for making it your life's mission to save, learn more and study this unique animal. And thank you for coming to the rescue of the real-life drama of Kenny the Tree Kangaroo, who found a comfortable spot in the plumbing department of our hardware store one Monday morning.

Go to this link to look at actual footage of Kenny, at Eacham Hardware, Malanda.

https://au.news.yahoo.com/kenny-tree-kangaroo-caught-stocking-055722637.html

Link to the Tree Roo Park and Conservation Centre:

https://www.treeroorescue.org.au/

ABOUT THE AUTHOR

As a contemporary romance author, Frances Dall'Alba loves nothing more than losing herself in a good romance. She's all about helping you forget the housework, or the bus to work you're going to miss, if you don't put the book down now!

She's devoted to giving her readers an emotional, yet satisfying ride, with a love story that'll melt your heart and keep the pages turning right until the end.

When she isn't writing, Frances is climbing mountains, searching for waterfalls and swimming across lakes. She loves to exercise, would prefer it if someone else cooked dinner every night, and never notices dust on the furniture.

She lives with her husband in tropical Far North Queensland, and uses her great baking skills to tempt her three daughters to visit home as often as they can.

Say hello to Frances

Visit her website http://francesdallalba.wixsite.com/ francesdallalba and subscribe to her newsletter. It will keep you up-to-date with:

- New releases
- Pre-order links
- New cover reveals and excerpts
- Exclusive member rewards
- And lots more!

Follow Frances on Facebook, Instagram, Bookbub and Goodreads. To do so, click on this link: https://linktr.ee/ francesdallalba

Still have a question?

Ask me at https://francesdallalba.wixsite.com/francesdallalba/contact

Leave a Review

Did you enjoy this book? The best favour you can do for an author is to leave a **review**. If you'd like to leave a review, go to your place of on-line purchase of the book, or search for the book on **Goodreads** and leave a review. Thank you.

Lightning Source UK Ltd.
Milton Keynes UK
UKHW010852030223
416423UK00001B/229